After completing a degree in journalism, then working in advertising and mothering her kids, **Robin Gianna** had what she calls her 'awakening'. She decided she wanted to write the romance novels she'd loved since her teens, and now enjoys pushing her characters towards their own happily-ever-afters. When she's not writing Robin fills her life with a happily messy kitchen, a needy garden, a wonderful husband, three great kids, a drooling bulldog and one grouchy Siamese cat.

Also by Robin Gianna

Changed by His Son's Smile
The Last Temptation of Dr Dalton
Flirting with Dr Off-Limits
It Happened in Paris...
Her Greek Doctor's Proposal
Her Christmas Baby Bump
The Prince and the Midwife
Reunited with His Runaway Bride
Baby Surprise for the Doctor Prince
The Spanish Duke's Holiday Proposal

Discover more at millsandboon.co.uk.

TEMPTED BY
THE BROODING
SURGEON

ROBIN GIANNA

MILLS & BOON

First published in Great Britain 2018
by Mills & Boon, an imprint of HarperCollins*Publishers*
1 London Bridge Street, London, SE1 9GF

Large Print edition 2018

© 2018 Robin Gianakopoulos

ISBN: 978-0-263-07311-9

MIX
Paper from
responsible sources
FSC www.fsc.org   FSC™ C007454

This book is produced from independently certified
FSC™ paper to ensure responsible forest management. For
more information visit www.harpercollins.co.uk/green.

Printed and bound in Great Britain
by CPI Group (UK) Ltd, Croydon, CR0 4YY

I'd like to thank Julie Niezgoda, MD, for her tremendous help as I learned about the medical missions she's participated in. She gave me heaps of helpful details about what's involved in paediatric anaesthesia and surgeries on those missions, which are often done with much less equipment than modern hospitals provide.

Appreciate it so much, Julie!

Smooches! xoxo

CHAPTER ONE

WHAT *CAN* GO wrong *will* go wrong.

Annabelle Richards had no idea who'd said that first but, boy, they sure were right. What should have been a ten-hour flight from Chicago to Lima, Peru, then another hour and a half travel to the mission hospital, had turned into a forty-eight-hour delay. She was finally in the back of a taxi, dead tired from lack of sleep and running late for what should have been the second day of her posting at the hospital but was now day one because of her delays. She was scheduled to start at 8:00 a.m. Just seven minutes away.

She leaned forward to ask the taxi driver the same question she'd already asked a dozen times. "Are we close?"

"*Sí*. Soon, *señorita*. Short minutes more."

Annabelle tried to relax back into the vinyl seat

of the dusty cab, but the tightness in her gut kept her sitting upright. The entire surgical team was likely already annoyed, her lateness interrupting their carefully designed schedule and putting everyone behind on attending to all the patients they'd hoped to see. She could only pray that the first surgery scheduled this morning wasn't something life-threatening.

What if someone died because she wasn't there in time to get them anesthetized and intubated? What if one of their small patients had gotten sicker yesterday while they'd waited for her, making today's surgeries even more serious?

How had everything gone so wrong all at the same time?

First, the transport monitor she'd worked months to have donated for this trip had gotten locked into a storage room that no one had seemed to have the key for. A frantic hour had gone by before she'd finally retrieved it, then torn to the airport, panicking that she'd miss her flight. Which, of course, she had. Then weather delays and missed connections added to the disaster.

Looking back, it was all her own stupid fault for being so determined to bring the monitor, instead of having it shipped. Except the whole reason she'd waited around to get it was because the last time she was here, a tiny premature baby had almost died without a monitor to check his heart rate and other vital signs.

She could only hope that missing a day of surgeries because of it hadn't resulted in a child dying anyway.

She scrubbed her hands down her cheeks, her nerves practically screaming with the need to finally get to the clinic. Being physically there and on time was more important than equipment any day.

Hadn't she been told more than once that her dog-with-a-bone determination got her into trouble sometimes? This sure was one of those times, and the trouble just kept coming. The huge delay had meant she'd also missed her meeting at the hospital in Lima. A beyond important meeting that might have saved her old school from being shut down in a matter of months. And now her dream to turn the school into a medical training facility for impoverished youths just might be doomed to failure.

Annabelle stared out the window at the passing landscape, wanting to distract herself before she went further into a panic spiral. The gorgeous, deep blue ocean and white sand beaches on one side below the road were in starkly colorful contrast to the green and brown mountains on the other side. Beautiful cliff-side homes and rickety shanties made of whatever hodgepodge of materials folks could get their hands on dotted the lush landscape.

The poverty in her old neighborhood was more than real. But in so many ways it couldn't compare to the tiny, leaky places so many people here in Peru called home. Whenever families heard the medical mission crews were coming to an area, they'd trek for miles, hoping their child would be chosen to receive surgery and care. They'd sleep on the ground and patiently line up for their children to be seen, and if they were told that their child couldn't be taken care of, that there was no more room in the schedule, they'd smile and thank the doctors and nurses, saying they'd be back to try again next time.

Helping those children was beyond important. Somehow, she had to find a way to get the meeting in Lima rescheduled so she could get the partnership and funding to give underprivileged kids a dream and a goal, while still taking care of as many patients needing surgery here as possible.

The taxi driver finally turned off the main road, and she sat up straight again, relief surging through her veins as she recognized the landscape. "Is this it? Are we about there?"

"*Sí.* Just up the hill a couple of miles."

Thank God.

The cab lurched to a stop where the road ended, which left another five hundred or so feet to the small hospital OR. On an uphill slope she knew wasn't easy to navigate, especially when it rained. "Just put my suitcase and the rest of the stuff on that rock there, please," she said, pointing. "I'll get it later."

He nodded and did as she asked before she stuffed a wad of money in his hand. Being in a position to give a generous tip to someone she knew needed it always awed her and thrilled her, after so many years of having nothing herself. "Thanks so much. Can you hand me the monitor so I can carry it easier?"

The sketchy Spanish she'd been painstakingly learning, along with a few gestures, seemed to get her message across and he deposited the equipment into her wide open arms with a grin and a nod. *"Adios."*

"Adios! Thanks again."

Annabel turned to trudge up the hill, slipping a little on small stones as she went. Had the path always been this long? Huffing and puffing and only about halfway there, it felt very possible that her arms might crack off from the heavy weight of the patient monitor before she even got to the operating room. If she'd had any brains, she should have paid the man extra money to carry it for her. But since she knew everyone was waiting for her to finally show up, pausing to put down the awkward thing and catch her breath wasn't an option.

Thrashing herself all over again for not thinking this through, Annabelle heaved the transport monitor higher against her chest, praying she didn't drop it before it could even be used. Wouldn't that just be the icing on the disaster cake?

Sweat rolled down her back, morphing from a trickle to a waterfall despite it being only about seventy degrees on an early March morning, and every hurried step seemed to add another pound to the weight in her arms. A few more lurching steps, and she topped the rise. Seeing the cement block building that made do as an operating room in this part of Peru would have her whooping if she'd had any breath left, but instead she sagged in relief.

She'd made it.

Trying hard to ignore the way the monitor jabbed her breasts and the sharply painful muscle twisting in her shoulder, she bit her lip to keep from cursing. Finally, she got the doorknob turned and the door shoved open with her shoulder.

"So sorry I'm late," she said breathlessly to anyone listening as she stumbled into the sparse room. "And that I missed yesterday, too. I hope you were able to take care of nonsurgical stuff since I wasn't here but, still, I know it wasn't good that I missed my flight. Really sorry about that."

Quickly scanning the space to take in the small assembly of medical professionals near the surgical bed, she saw the familiar face of a Peruvian nurse named Karina whom she'd worked with here before, and her friend, Jen, who worked in a different hospital in Chicago.

"Hi!" Annabelle said with a smile and an accompanying wave of her few free fingers. The lack of return smiles, along with the worry on their faces, briefly registered before she looked down at the small patient they were crowded around, who was lying on the bed and staring up at her somberly.

"Hello, buddy!"

She sent him a reassuring grin before looking for a table close enough to the patient to set the monitor down, her arms beyond desperate to be relieved of the heavy machine.

"Oh, my gosh, this thing weighs a ton! Where can I put it? I hope you all haven't been waiting for me too long. Getting here has been one problem after another! First there was a delay getting the monitor at the hospital, which made me miss my stupid flight. Then I hit bad weather and missed my connection, which was even worse. Plus, I had no idea airport security would take such a crazy long time examining the monitor this morning, and I—"

"Most of our surgeries have been done without a monitor in the past. If security had a problem with it, you should have left it at the airport. Or shipped it to begin with, which would have prevented all your problems so you could be here on time."

Annabelle froze, her heart knocked hard against her ribs, and suddenly she couldn't breathe at all.

That voice. The cold tone. The stinging criticism. All were too horrifyingly familiar. Forcing herself to slowly turn toward the tall, gowned man standing with his arms folded across his chest next to the patient, her worst fears were confirmed.

She may not have seen him for five years, but she'd recognize those hard brown eyes anywhere. The cut cheekbones. The bronzed skin. The displeasure and disdain on his face. The lips that were inexplicably sensuously shaped, even when pressed together in clear annoyance.

Dr. Daniel Ferrera in the flesh.

The man who had sabotaged her first career goals.

Gulping, she tried to pull air into her lungs. How could this be? How was it possible that of all the cardiac surgeons in the whole world, he was the one here on this mission trip in Peru?

"Making us miss an entire day of surgeries yesterday was unfair to everyone else, both the patients and the surgical team who took valuable vacation time to be here, Dr. Richards. And this morning you've kept the patient waiting for his surgery, making it so fewer patients will get seen today and all week, disappointing the families hoping their child will be taken care of since we won't be able to fit in nearly as many because of your actions."

Condemnation filled his dark eyes as they seared into hers. "I could have sent someone to get the monitor from the airport later, while you were here doing your job, but apparently some things never change."

"I... The monitor was donated by a benefactor."

"And the benefactor is more important than our patients here?"

"No. No, of course not. But I had to make sure the monitor arrived safely. When I was here last, we almost lost a patient because there was no monitor. A premature infant, and that's just not acceptable if there's any way to avoid it. So I decided to bring one here this time." Icy shock numbed her brain, making it hard to speak coherently, and her insides seemed to squeeze and sag along with her arms under the heavy weight of the monitor as she stared at him.

Daniel must have seen her struggling to hold the machine, as a disgusted sound left his lips before he strode to take it from her, sliding it onto a nearby metal table.

"If you'd simply shipped it, you wouldn't have hit bad weather, wouldn't have missed your connection, wouldn't have had to deal with airport security and wouldn't have missed your first day, setting back the schedule for the whole week. It seems apparent that you're not cut out for this kind of work."

The arrogant tone, the sarcastically raised dark eyebrow, the scorn on his face cut through her horrified paralysis. Yes, it was true, she might not be cut out for any of the things she'd striven so hard to be excellent at. She wasn't like him and all the others who came from their hoity-toity privileged backgrounds, people who'd had every advantage handed to them with white gloves and smiles, showered with accolades and money and a golden path laid out for them to become physicians.

She might be leagues below him in every way but, if nothing else, her pathetic history had at least given her grit and bravado. Living in rough neighborhoods around even rougher people had taught her that, when pushed, you'd better push back or you'd end up rubbed into the floor. She wasn't about to let him talk to her that way, in front of their patient and the rest of the small surgical staff, whether she deserved it or not.

"For your information, this is my ninth mission trip, Dr. Ferrera. I'm not a newbie. I know the circumstances we're dealing with here. But if we can save even one life by having a monitor, I was damned well going to make that happen." She grabbed the mask and IV with shaking hands to show him it was time to stop talking and get to work. "I'm no longer the green anesthesiologist I was when we last worked together. Since your insults and criticism are only delaying the surgery on this boy even longer, I suggest we get to it."

Dark eyes slashed across her like a whip before he turned to the patient and crew. "Since Dr. Richards obviously hasn't had a chance to study our surgery lineup today, I'll have to go over it again. We have an atrial septal defect, with the hole thankfully small. Get him hooked up to the all-important monitor while Dr. Richards gets the gases ready. As soon as he's asleep and ready, I'll get started."

Everyone got to work. Daniel's scowl and his stiff professional tone changed completely as he leaned over the little boy, speaking softly and melodically in Spanish. Whatever he said actually made the child smile, and though Annabelle didn't want to feel the squishiness in her heart at how beautifully he was reassuring their young patient, it happened anyway.

How could the man be such a chameleon? A total autocratic jerk one minute, and a gentle, caring doctor the next? It didn't matter, really. Neither of them would ever get past what had happened five years ago, and his obviously negative convictions about her skills. The thought of having to work with him for two entire weeks made her stomach churn. Before she'd even started her first surgery, she found herself hoping it was the fastest two-week mission trip in history.

But with no way to actually warp time to make that happen, she would focus on their patient and her job. She prepared to connect the two anesthetic gases to the small clear mask, then leaned over to show it to the child. Trying to explain it to him in her halting Spanish, she realized the stress of facing Daniel Ferrera seemed to have obliterated from her brain the few words she did know in the other language. With the surgery needing to start pronto, she knew that swallowing her pride was the right thing to do, and turned to her friend Karina. "Can you tell him I'm going to put the mask over his nose and mouth, and he'll go to dreamland for a while?"

Before Karina could say a word, Daniel Ferrera leaned over the patient again, speaking more of that lovely, lilting Spanish, and mere seconds after Annabelle placed the mask on his face, the boy's eyes were closed. Grateful that she'd done this enough times that her shakiness evaporated as she worked through the steps, Annabelle worked to connect the IV lines to his arms and legs, then the final, central line to his neck connecting directly to his heart. A necessary step of stunning the heart before the surgery could begin. "Pressure?"

"Monitor shows we have railroad tracks so all okay," Jennifer said.

Annabelle glanced at the monitor, glad to have it for confirmation, no matter what Daniel Ferrera thought about it. "Good." She concentrated on inserting a breathing tube, relieved that the boy's mouth opened wide enough for it to go in easily. "Neuromuscular blockade set. We have a one airway, so he's breathing manually."

All she got was a nod from Daniel Ferrera before he got to work. Just as she'd remembered from the last time she'd watched him perform a delicate operation, he was steady, confident and precise. Not a single bobble or pause, just an even pace and periodic questions to the support crew and her as they monitored the patient. But there was no question that the tone of voice he used when he talked to her was completely different than the one he used with everyone else. Abrupt and clipped, showing loud and clear that he was still annoyed.

What was with the man that he couldn't just let things go? It was clear nothing had changed from five years ago. Didn't he believe people deserved a second chance after a mistake? Even if that mistake had been a terrible one?

For the next several hours, the surgery went smoothly, the whole team working together seamlessly without a hitch.

"That's a wrap." Daniel said, finally leaning back and running his finger down the closed incision. "Time for epinephrine to get the heart working again, then we'll wake him, Dr. Richards."

Her eyes lifted to briefly meet his, and if that icy blue could have physically stabbed him, he had a feeling she would have been glad. One of the many personality traits he disliked in medical professionals was if they tried to pass the buck when something went wrong. He did everything he could to make sure every surgery went perfectly, but when he made an error, or an error was made by someone he was supervising, he owned it.

Which Annabelle Richards should do, as far as he was concerned. Maybe her lateness hadn't caused catastrophic damage, but they very well might not be able to perform surgery on all the patients they had scheduled today without everyone working into the late hours. Her tardiness wasn't fair to any of their small patients who might have to wait until the next visit, or to the hardworking staff at this hospital who were donating their time to this cause.

"Are you prepared to work late tonight, if we have to, Dr. Richards? You look a little tired from your stressful travels."

"How sweet of you to worry about me, Dr. Ferrera," she said in a sarcastic tone. "No need, though. I may look like a hag, but I'm not tired at all. I'll work as late as is needed."

"Good. Because now we're more than a day behind schedule, as you know."

"I do know." A near snarl curled her lip as she turned back to the equipment.

Hag? Now, that was a word no one could ever apply to Annabelle Richards, curled lip or not. Daniel studied the mutinous expression on her face as she diligently avoided looking at him, and couldn't deny that, for some reason, her take-no-prisoners attitude and spunk was as appealing as the sweet smile in her blue eyes and on her lush lips that appeared as she turned to their small patient. He couldn't deny that, for a split second, thoughts of what it would feel like to kiss that seductive mouth had scorched his brain just as it had the first time he'd seen her five years ago. It annoyed the hell out of him.

Gorgeous, sexy and sassy didn't have anything to do with good medical skills, and he figured that her beauty had probably helped her advance in her career when she shouldn't have. When he'd blocked her getting a permanent position five years ago at the hospital where he still worked, two of the upper-level hospital administrators had stepped in and gone to bat for her. He still believed her good looks, with serious curves in all the right places, had been part of why they'd wanted to keep her around.

Regardless, Daniel was the best cardiac surgeon at the hospital, and when he'd stated with no room for discussion that he'd never work with her again, they'd known he'd meant it. No one wanted to have to dance around that kind of scheduling nightmare, so off she'd gone in a matter of weeks.

Had he thought about her a few times afterward? For whatever reason, he couldn't deny that he had. For a few months after she'd left, when he'd closed his eyes at night, he'd sometimes seen her face and lips. Her silky blond hair falling to her shoulders in soft waves. That body of hers, which any man would salivate over. He didn't think the strangeness of his random thoughts about her were from any guilt over getting her fired. No, he'd figured it must be a sign that he'd been working too hard. Needed to let off steam with someone he knew was interested in only that and not any other kind of relationship, since he could never offer anything long term.

Yes, he'd thought about Annabelle Richards, but had he ever regretted blocking her from getting the permanent position? Not for one second. There was no room for error in surgery. He knew that better than anyone, and on the rare occasions he got pushback from someone on his medical team for his perfectionist attitudes, he thought of his brother and stood his ground.

His brother's cardiac surgeon simply hadn't been careful enough during the delicate surgery he'd needed, and if he had been, Gabriel would still be here, joking with Daniel, pushing the boundaries with their parents and grandparents, living his life at one hundred percent velocity like he always had until the day he'd died.

The loss had torn Daniel up. Had left a painful, gaping hole in his family, and he had no desire to ever forget how that felt.

Remembering his brother gave him the strength and resolution to be the kind of surgeon he had to be. To insist that everyone be on top of their game for every single patient. Every single time. He and his team owed it to his patients, and to the people who loved them, to give every one of them the best possible care available, and that included the nursing staff and the anesthesiologist.

The patient Dr. Annabelle Richards had nearly killed five years ago during surgery had suffered from exactly the same heart condition as Gabriel. No way had he wanted her to work as the anesthesiologist on his team.

And yet here she was. So what was he going to do about it? Mission hospital or not, he owed every single patient the best surgical outcome he could obtain with the tools that he had at hand. Dr. Annabelle Richards would not be the person who lowered that standard.

Daniel yanked down his surgical mask, gave their patient one more careful check over, asked him if he felt okay, and reassured him that he'd be visiting with him in Recovery when he felt better. Stripping off his gloves, he moved out of the OR to see the next patient coming in. He checked the diagnostic work and the seriousness of the six-month-old's situation. Stuck his head into the small, spartan waiting room crammed with patients before talking with the local woman juggling the surgery schedule to see how many children they could see that day.

Whoever the anesthesiologist was on each mission, they often accompanied him on these quick rounds. But Dr. Richards had chosen to stay back in the OR, probably to tinker with her all-important monitor.

Having her work as anesthesiologist for the next few days' surgeries was the only option to ensure that everyone on the docket got taken care of. But as soon as he had a moment free? He'd be looking for a replacement for Annabelle Richards.

CHAPTER TWO

DAWN CREPT MISTILY across the mountains as Daniel stepped outside the hotel where the medical team was staying, sipping hot coffee obtained from the large urn in the foyer. He savored the taste of it on his tongue, letting the flavor of the locally grown arabica linger there, along with memories of his childhood. He and his brother had always loved the stuff, and he smiled, remembering sending Gabriel to sneak into the kitchen in the morning to pour both of them a cup, heaping them with cream and sugar.

Daniel had been more of a rule follower than his twin, but when it had been to his benefit, he'd been happy to take advantage of his brother's mischievous, more daring nature. Sometimes that had involved sports and adventures, sometimes it had been stealing desserts or coffee or other things they weren't supposed to have, straight from under their nanny's or parents' noses.

He took another swig of the hot brew. Straight black was the way he liked it now, giving him a much-needed caffeine jolt after having worked late into the night before getting busy making phone calls to acquaintances at various hospitals who might know of an accomplished anesthesiologist who'd be available and willing to work at the mission hospital for the next two weeks.

With any luck one of the people recommended would be willing to take over Annabelle Richards's small shoes. He knew she'd be furious and, to his complete surprise, a niggle of discomfort over his phone calls briefly poked at him, knowing she'd given her vacation time to this trek and gone through a lot of effort to get here against the odds. There was also the undeniable fact that throughout yesterday's surgeries she'd been utterly competent and professional.

But that didn't mean that she always would be. He had no idea if she'd grown as a doctor, and he reminded himself, again, that it was critical to have only the best anesthesiologist available for the kinds of complicated heart surgeries they performed here.

But maybe there was some compromise to be found. Maybe he should suggest she work in a different mission while she was in Peru, rather than sending her back to the United States when he found a replacement. There were several clinics in poor parts of the country that were only occasionally open to patients. Clinics that did far less complicated surgeries than he'd be doing. Surgeries that didn't take six or eight hours to accomplish, and weren't life-threatening. She could handle those kinds of things, he knew. And any local doctor without much in the way of staff would welcome her help.

It was a good plan. And maybe part of the reason it sounded good to him was because he couldn't deny that, despite having very valid reasons, seeing anger and maybe hurt in those blue eyes that could quickly turn from warm and friendly to icy disdain in a single blink wasn't something he looked forward to. Maybe knowing another clinic needed her would make her happy to go there instead.

Impatient with himself and the odd mental discomfort he felt, Daniel looked out towards the mountains in the distance, pondering how he could get Dr. Richards moved to another clinic, when a movement nearby caught his attention. As though he'd conjured her from the shadowy mist, Annabelle came out of the hotel doors, her pale hair shimmering through the mist much the way the moon was, still hanging low in the slowly lightening sky.

Surprised that she'd be up so early after her botched travels and long work day, he took in the light pink robe she wore, cinched close at the waist and emphasizing her large breasts and the roundness of her hips. Her legs, bare and shapely, seemed longer than when she wore scrubs. Both hands were wrapped around a steaming cup of coffee, and the way she breathed in the scent, closed her eyes as she took a sip, and tipped her head back as it slid down her throat, made his heart give a little kick. A small smile tipped her soft-looking lips. His entire body reacted to the utter sensuous pleasure on the woman's face.

This was how she'd look making love. Pleasured, satisfied, wanting more. And he wanted to give it to her. Wanted to walk over, kiss her and open up that robe to slide his hands inside to feel her soft skin, caress all those curves.

Damn. Where had all that come from? Somehow, he forced himself to look away and take a big gulp of his own coffee. His chest burned, but he wasn't sure it was from the drink. Thinking of her in that way was all kinds of wrong when they were working together, even if it ended up being for only a short time.

Daniel didn't know whether to try to skulk deeper into the shadows until she went back inside or make some noise to let her know he was out here. He decided the first was cowardly and weak, and since he tried to never be either of those things, he took a few steps toward her.

"I see you need coffee to get going in the morning as much as I do."

She swung to stare at him, surprise touching

her face before it settled into a frown. The pleasure replaced by annoyance. "I like coffee, but I don't need it to get going."

"Energetic the second you leap from bed? Lucky you."

"Not exactly, but I do other things to wake myself up."

"Now you've intrigued me." Which was an understatement, as several completely inappropriate thoughts lunged into his head. "What things?"

"I'm always amazed at how beautiful it is up here," she said, ignoring his question to look out over the vista in front of them. "You're from Peru originally, aren't you? How did you end up in Philadelphia?"

He let his gaze follow hers to the mountains and the golden rays illuminating their peaks. "This was home for us until I was ten years old. Still is a part of me, I guess. We lived in a more urban area, which was, and is, beautiful in its own way. But the government became corrupt, and rival terror groups wreaked havoc on the entire country. The political unrest and economic mess finally forced my parents to move to the US, taking some of the family business interests with them."

"I'd heard about the political troubles, but it's much better now, isn't it?"

"Yes, thank God. My grandparents stayed, and there were a number of years that we worried about their safety. But the government and economy are both good now, and businesses are thriving. The quality of life is good, too, for many. But that can't be said for everyone here, as you already know."

"Why is that?" As soon as she said it, her lips twisted. "Never mind. The same question can be asked about the US and plenty of other places. Why there are those who have a lot and others who don't."

It seemed her blue eyes shadowed at that, and he nodded. "Yes. The stark contrasts that exist here are part of the wonder of Peru, and part of its shame. Until I moved away, I took for granted the huge and interesting differences between the arid coastline and deep rainforests. Snow-covered mountains and the fertile valleys that grow so many fruits and vegetables, sugarcane and coffee. Gold and silver mines are a big part of the economy, too, and I'm sure you've seen our famous and unique fabric arts. So much to love about this place, and for tourists to enjoy."

"Do the indigenous people resent the tourists showing up at Machu Picchu and their villages, or do they appreciate the tourist trade? The foreigners buying the gorgeous woven clothes and blankets?"

"I assume they're glad to sell their wares and to make money that way, but don't know for sure. I haven't really talked to patients' families about that—guess I should." Interesting that she'd asked that question, when he hadn't really thought about it at all. "Peruvians have a deep history with so many ancient cultures and widely diverse ethnicities. There's also a sharp divide between the wealthy elite, like my own family, and the extremely poor that I'm committed to take care of."

"So you're one of the wealthy elite? Somehow that doesn't surprise me."

The way she said it, with a slight scowl creasing her brow, showed she wasn't the least impressed by his background. "I am blessed in that way, yes. But it doesn't blind me to the problems here. To the atrocious wall in Lima that runs between shantytowns on one side of the mountain and large homes with every amenity on the other."

"The wall of shame. It's awful." She scrunched up her face in a way that would have been beyond cute if the subject weren't so serious. "But even though that kind of divide isn't as physically obvious up here and in other places in the world, the gap is still pretty big. I mean, look at this place."

He didn't have to follow the wave of her hand to know what she meant. "True. Sometimes I feel guilty to be staying in this kind of modern hotel, knowing that, close by, some of the families we take care of don't have running water or electricity."

"Me, too. But does it make me a horrible person

that I'm glad to be able to stay here anyway? I've worked in places that didn't have running water and had generators that only provided electricity part of the day, but I can't lie. I appreciate knowing I can at least take a shower and that's what keeps bringing me back to stay more often when I'm working here."

He had to smile at her earnest expression, as though she felt she really should feel guilty about that. "No, it doesn't make you a horrible person. It makes you someone from the Western world, and we're all spoiled by having a light switch we can just turn on, aren't we?"

"Yeah. If the electric bill's been paid," she murmured, before sending him a slightly strained smile. "Anyway, I think I'll get going on my morning routine then take advantage of that shower before work."

"Surgery doesn't start for another couple of hours. Why are you up so early, after having so little sleep because you had to bring that monitor?"

That earned him a narrow-eyed stare, and he

mentally smacked himself for bringing it up again. And why had he? He'd been thinking about the gray smudges beneath her pretty eyes, wishing she'd go back to bed for a while so she'd feel refreshed. Not about the stupid monitor or her lateness.

"I'm always up early. It's important to get mentally centered before taking on the tasks of the day."

"What do you do to get mentally centered?"

"Meditation. Yoga. I know…" She held up her hand. "Someone like you is probably thinking I don't have a yoga body, but a person doesn't have to be thin to do healthy stretching, you know."

Her words sent his gaze back to her tantalizing figure in that robe and he had to yank it away before she saw him staring. "Someone like me?"

"Yes. A person who thinks it's his right to judge and criticize others. How they do their job. Where they come from or what they wear. Mostly, it's obvious you usually decide that pretty much everyone on your medical teams come up short, undeserving of breathing the same rarefied air as you."

"You have me all wrong." Inexplicably, her words stung, even as he felt confused as to why she was saying some of it. "I don't judge people. Didn't we just have a conversation about how much I care about the have-nots who live here? As for my medical teams, I demand the best for my patients. That was the only thing on my mind five years ago, since that's clearly what you're talking about here."

"I want the best for my patients, too. Except I don't throw other people under the bus, even when they make a mistake or could do something better. I give them a second chance, and try to help them along the way."

"Some patients never get a second chance." The words came out more sharply than he'd intended as memories of Gabriel squeezed his chest. "Which is why I insist on working with only the most qualified people, instead of pandering to anyone's ego."

"Well, anyone who could keep their ego intact

around you must be made of steel. And it seems to me that maybe you're the one with the ego problem. Hotshot cardiac surgeon from a wealthy family. A guy with a God complex who thinks he's better than everyone else."

"I have many colleagues who ask to work with me, and if that's because they think I'm one of the best surgeons around, I'm happy about that. If you call that a big ego, so be it."

She took a swig of coffee and shrugged. "I call it like I see it."

He took a step closer, his chest burning at her unexpected attack, and after they'd had such a friendly conversation, too. "Maybe the truth is you have a plenty big ego yourself. Attractive enough to land a job in a prestigious hospital. Beautiful enough to have hospital higher-ups go to bat for you, even when you mess up."

She gasped, taking two big steps forward to jab her finger into his chest, her eyes flashing with blue fury. "That's just insulting, and if I were a man you wouldn't dare say something like that to me. I'm not going to stand here and defend myself, because I couldn't care less what you think about me, other than you have to trust me to do a good job here. You believe what you want about anything else, but I know what I'm doing, and I got my job through hard work and nothing else. You're stuck working with me and I'm stuck working with you for the next two weeks. We have children to heal and lives to save, and that's the only thing that's important to me. So get over yourself and deal with it."

She swung around and marched to the door. Coffee sloshed from her cup and onto her pink sleeve, trickling to the ground, but she just kept going without another look back.

Daniel blew out a slow breath as he watched the sexy sway of her backside disappear through the door. How had he lost control of that conversation, and why had he let her goad him into verbalizing his questions about why some of the hospital administrators had argued to keep her on?

Normally, he was a man who could hold his thoughts, but there was something about her that got under his skin. He wasn't sure what it was, but he'd felt so frustrated at her words, and at the same time he'd been mesmerized by her lips as they'd moved, that the comments about her beauty helping her get her job had just fallen out of his mouth, even as he'd known he shouldn't say anything. Even as he'd spoken, a part of him had wanted to reach for her, grasp her shoulders, and pull her against him. Wanted to drop his mouth to hers to keep her from lambasting him. Wanted to sip the coffee from her lips, experience the taste of her that he knew would be sweeter than the sugar in her drink.

And wouldn't that have been a giant mistake? What the hell was wrong with him?

He rubbed his hand down his face. The number one priority in dealing with her just became being careful to speak to her, and react to her, with only the utmost professionalism. How ironic would it be for her to lodge a complaint against *him* about his conduct on this medical mission?

A brisk walk might help him get his equilibrium back. And maybe it was time for him to learn to do a little meditation himself, to purge his brain of any and all peculiar and troubling thoughts about Annabelle Richards.

Another long day of surgeries left Daniel with an aching back and a sense of satisfaction. The hours spent were worth a little discomfort, since repairing holes in children's small hearts or addressing hypoplastic left heart syndrome and other critical heart malformations was exactly why he did these missions.

The whole team had worked tirelessly along with him, including Annabelle. He couldn't deny that she'd shown herself to be a steady hand with the anesthesia, communicating well with the nurses and bringing what he'd learned was her special brand of charm to the young patients. She might not speak very good Spanish but at least she tried, and knew how to deal with their patients in a way that calmed even the most nervous. Her wide smile, and the way she used tiny fairy and superhero dolls as props to leap gently onto their little arms and bodies, distracting them from the medical preparation happening around them, always made them relax and laugh before she got down to the serious business of getting them to sleep for surgery.

Maybe she really had grown as a doctor over the past five years, after the anesthesia resident's nearly catastrophic error and her mistake of not supervising well enough what the guy was doing. An error that had nearly ended up with their young patient dead. Maybe he wouldn't have been as angry if the teen hadn't been having the same surgery Gabriel had died from, or maybe it wouldn't have made any difference at all. But he had to believe that not a soul alive would blame him for being furious and distraught about a member of his staff nearly losing a child's life through completely avoidable actions.

It was hard for him to think beyond that upsetting day when it came to Annabelle. Hard to give her the benefit of the doubt now, his chest still constricting at the memory of the chaos as they'd struggled to keep the boy alive. Another teenager, this one under Daniel's watch, nearly dying. Was he supposed to just look the other way? Forget about it? The boy's family had no idea how close they'd come to losing him that day, a fate that would have changed their world forever.

Some would say he should move on and give Annabelle another chance since she was older and more experienced now. And maybe they'd be right. But he'd already gotten the wheels greased for him to work with a new doc, and for her to do other, still important, work but at a different clinic, far away from him. He would feel under less stress in the OR here, and patients at the new clinic would get Annabelle's help facilitating the surgeries they needed. So nothing but good would come from his plan.

"You got this?" he asked the team after the patient's vital signs were normal and he was satisfied the surgery was a success.

"Yes, Dr. Ferrera," Annabelle said in a cool, professional voice. "Ready to remove the breathing tube and IVs."

"Good. I'll be over at Administration, evaluating tomorrow's patients, making final decisions about who's on the list and when."

Annabelle and the nurses all nodded, focusing on the patient, as they should. Daniel stripped off his gloves and mask and went to the other cement block building that served their bare-bones administration staff and doubled as a wait-ing room/sleeping room combo. Families with children sat on the folding chairs and sprawled on the floor, many of whom he knew had come from miles away. Patiently waiting to be seen, they slept there or outside on homemade blan-kets they'd brought with them, along with bags of food, since the clinic could only provide bottled water to drink. They waited to find out if they'd be one of those chosen to get well, or be put on the list for the next time a clinic was run. Some looked deceptively healthy, others were visibly ill. Far too thin, too pale, too quiet and motion-less for a child to be.

Daniel's own heart abnormality had always been hidden behind a facade of good health. He'd played sports, he'd skied, he'd seemed fine in every way. With both their heart functions in reasonably good and manageable conditions, it had been decided that surgery on the identical twins wasn't worth the risk to either of them. That was, until Gabriel's heart condition had worsened and he'd ended up needing the surgery that had ultimately killed him.

Daniel hadn't had to face that.

He knew it was possible that things might change. The hole in his heart that both brothers had been born with, and that medical professionals had always kept an eye on, could get larger and more problematic than the simple arrhythmia he had to deal with sometimes. Living with his heart abnormality was a little like carrying around a ticking bomb. It might never go off. Or it could someday result in endocarditis or sepsis. Stroke. Death.

It meant Daniel lived every day as if it were his last and never committed to a forever. No long-term relationships, no children. He simply couldn't promise anyone that he'd be here on earth for a long time, and it wouldn't be fair to put a woman or a family through that kind of uncertainty. Through the possibility of future pain.

Twenty years had passed since his brother had died, and time had dulled the intense grief. He and his parents and grandparents still dealt with the kind of deep pain that came from a sudden, shocking loss. The ache would always be there.

Holding in a deep sigh, he moved his gaze from the throngs of patiently waiting families to the front desk, trying to detach himself by focusing on the list of patients there. He shoved down the ache that came with every mission trip, knowing he couldn't fix everyone who needed it. Knowing that his decisions about who would get on the surgery lists and who wouldn't meant more worries for the people who loved them. More kids who couldn't play in a normal way until their hearts were repaired. More who might die if the tests done before he'd arrived didn't show how serious their situation really was. More whose families might lose them forever if he made the wrong choice.

"May I have the list of possible patients for tomorrow?" he asked the receptionist. With the long sheet in hand, he moved from family to family, child to child. Reading their charts and talking with them about their symptoms. Listening to their hearts to evaluate murmurs and arrhythmias, and to figure out the best course of action to help them to get better.

Hoping and praying he got it all right.

"I think that's it for the day," he said in Spanish to the clinic receptionist, who seemed as worn out as he did, and he knew the whole team had to feel the same way. "I'll let everyone know we're done until tomorrow morning."

"*Sí*, Dr. Ferrera. I'm sure more folks will arrive by morning, and I'll try to sort them by health priority before you talk with them after surgery tomorrow."

"Be sure to let me know if any seem critical, and I'll look at them between patients to see if they need to be fitted into the rotation as soon as possible."

She nodded, and Daniel bit back a tired sigh at the thought of more patients to evaluate even before the medical team started surgery in the morning. But that was the whole reason they were here, wasn't it? To see the maximum number of the most ill children was the name of the game.

When Daniel stepped back inside the cement block building that housed the OR, he was surprised to see Annabelle helping Jennifer and Karina wash out the masks and tracheal tubes they'd used for their patients, sterilizing them, then hanging them to dry. Most docs left that to the nursing staff and local tech assistants, and he watched her lean over to dig out surgical items like sponges and syringes from a box he hadn't seen before.

"What's all that stuff in there, and where did it come from?" he asked.

"I brought it." Annabelle didn't look up at him, just kept laying out items for tomorrow morning's surgeries.

"Did your hospital donate it?"

"Dr. Richards started a—"

Annabelle sent Jennifer a deep frown, accompanied by a small shake of her head, that had Jennifer quickly closing her mouth.

What was that all about? He looked from Annabelle to Jennifer, then back to see Annabelle intensely concentrating on sorting the equipment. He couldn't help but wonder what it was that she clearly didn't want him to hear, and he would definitely be asking Jennifer later when Annabelle wasn't around to shush her.

"It's just a few things. Not as much as we'd like to have, but I didn't have much room in my suitcase and, of course, I had to bring the *useless* monitor."

So she was still angry with him about that. Not that it was any real surprise.

"I never said it was useless. I said we'd functioned without monitors plenty of times in the past, and that missing a whole day of surgeries, then being late with a patient already on the operating table and putting us hugely behind schedule, wasn't worth the time wasted getting one here."

As soon as he finished speaking, the strident

sound of his words made him feel a little ridiculous. It was history at this point, and the woman had worked hard all day with the rest of the team, with successful outcomes for every patient. He nearly opened his mouth to say something more, maybe a general congratulations and thank-you to the whole team, but the words died at the icy dislike in the look she sent him.

Those pretty lips of hers had thinned, too, but she didn't respond, which he was fine with as the subject needed to be dropped. "Anyway," he continued, annoyed that he felt awkward, "I'm told dinner is being held for us at the hotel. Anything I can do to help get things finished up here?"

"We're fine, Dr. Ferrera. Not much more to do, but you go ahead," Annabelle said as she hung another washed-out mask on the line.

"I'm not going to eat while you're all still out here."

"This is the last bit," Jennifer said, drying her hands and shooting him a grin. "And I don't know about anybody else, but I'm pretty much starving."

"Me, too," Daniel said, glad that at least she and the other nurse weren't holding some kind of grudge against him, channeling Annabelle's obvious dislike. He needed a good working relationship with the surgical team. "Let's go."

Normally on these kinds of trips Daniel had dinner with the team then excused himself to be alone. To regroup and relax after a long day of work that was stressful no matter how many years he'd been doing it, knowing children's lives were literally in his hands. But tonight the jovial mood and banter between the group kept him in his seat. Jennifer and Karina told a number of absurd hospital stories during dinner that had everyone laughing, including Annabelle. Why he found his attention was focused on her more than the storytellers, he wasn't sure. But as soon as he pondered that, the answer was obvious. Something about her sparkling eyes and infectious smile and pretty face made him smile, too. Drew him to her, whether he liked it or not.

From the moment they'd all started eating he couldn't help but notice that Annabelle seemed to enjoy her dinner far more than the rest of them. While the food at this hotel wasn't bad compared to what was often on the menu on mission trips, it hardly qualified as something to lick your lips over. But from the look on Annabelle's face as she ate every bite on her plate, anyone would have thought it was gourmet fare.

He nearly commented on it, but decided that would probably just make her mad at him all over again. His relationships with women might be of the sweet but short variety but that didn't mean he wasn't well aware that most females didn't appreciate observations about how much food they did or didn't eat, and whether or not they seemed to be enjoying it.

So he kept his mouth shut, while watching her pretty lips smile as she chewed and her enthusiasm as she poked another bite into her mouth. Enjoying watching her was a big part of the reason he hadn't retired to his room. Irritated though they'd both been with one another yesterday and this morning, he liked seeing her face relaxed and smiling, to hear the sound of her musical laughter. All that was a lot better than the scowl and cold voice she usually sent his way, though he didn't understand why he suddenly seemed to care about that.

"How about you, Annabelle?" The question came out of his mouth before he'd known he was going to ask it. "What's your most memorable mission trip story?"

Her eyes met his, looking surprised that he'd directed a question to her. "Hmm…" she said, tapping her finger against those lush lips. "I guess the craziest thing that ever happened was on one of my trips to Guatemala. The military guides in front of us were stopped, then surrounded, by a bunch of cutthroat-looking guys with all kinds of weapons pointed at them, and us," she began, and Daniel had to wonder why she was smiling at the retelling of what had to have been a scary situation. He'd been in a few himself, and even now would definitely not have been grinning about them.

"Oh, my heavens," Jennifer said, wide-eyed

as she pressed her hands to her cheeks. "What happened?"

"We were in the SUV behind them, and obviously we were worried. A nurse and I were the only passengers in the car, planning to meet the surgeon at the mission site. We kind of froze, wondering what our guides were going to do, figuring we should stay put. But then the guys came back to our car and gestured for us to get out. Gotta tell you, my knees were shaking! They took us to a house, and we had no idea what was going to happen. Whether they were going to take us in there and just plain shoot us, or do something awful to us, or what."

Daniel found he was holding his breath, even as he knew this story must have a good outcome or she wouldn't be smiling like she was.

"And?" Karina asked, obviously as riveted to hear the answer as he felt.

"They opened the door, and before we were even inside, we could hear a woman moaning. The minute we saw her, it was obvious that she was in labor and having some kind of serious problem. In a lot of pain. We ended up doing an emergency C-section on her, delivering the most beautiful twins you've ever seen. And they were healthy and fine—such a relief because we weren't sure what to expect, you know? Then later, when she and the babies were stable, I came back out to tell them everything was okay, that mama and babies were all fine and healthy. They whooped and hollered and hugged me and swung me around until I couldn't breathe!

"And one man—I never knew for sure, but I assume it was the babies' father—had tears rolling down his cheeks as he hugged me. It was an incredible feeling to know we'd helped, and that maybe the mother and babies wouldn't have made it without us. It felt like it was divine intervention that we were traveling there when they needed us, you know? It was the best day of my life."

"I can't believe you never told me this before!" Jennifer said. "So they were nice to you, then?"

"Maybe too nice." Annabelle grinned. "They plied us with rum and beer and all kinds of food, and we ended up staying the night there, partly because we wanted to check on the new mom and babies in the morning and partly because the military guys and our driver had a bit too much for them to handle getting behind the wheel."

"Wow, now that's one for the books," Karina said, laughing.

"Yeah, it was scary, but funny and wonderful, too. If we hadn't been on the road there at that moment, I think the outcome might have been bad. So it was a truly great night. The best feeling in the world. Then word apparently got around, because on the way to the two clinics we worked on that trip, there were always locals helping us out any way they could, even acting as secondary escorts along with the military. It was awesome to feel appreciated that way, and to know that we'd really made a difference there."

"When was this?" Karina asked.

"My first mission trip. Four years ago."

"Your very first one?" Jennifer exclaimed. "I'd imagine having such a scary experience might have made you think twice about going on another one."

"Life can be pretty scary in the US too. Can't let it keep you from living."

Jennifer nodded, and Daniel detected a trace of sympathy aimed at Annabelle as all amusement left both their faces. He figured they must be thinking of some of the violence, especially in big cities, that sent people to the ER no matter where they lived.

She quickly changed the subject to more mundane conversation about the hospitals where she and Jennifer worked, and he only half listened as he thought about Annabelle. Her first mission trip had been only four years ago, and she'd told him…what? That this was her ninth one? That was a lot of vacation time taken for this kind of trip. Most women he knew from both Peru and the US who had the means preferred taking spa vacations or trips to exotic locations. Just as he was about to ask her where else she'd gone on mission trips, and why, his cell phone rang.

He glanced down and nearly cursed when he saw it was the general surgeon from a Lima hospital that he'd asked to open the currently closed clinic near Huancayo for the duration of this trip. Not a conversation he wanted to have in front of everyone.

"Excuse me a moment," he said, getting up to stride to the hotel door. As he did so, he swore he could feel Annabelle's blue eyes drilling a hole in his back, but of course that was his imagination.

"Thanks for calling, Eduardo. So, are you able to take a week or so to work in Huancayo?"

"Good timing from this end. I can be there the day after tomorrow, with Alan Velasco coming to do anesthesia with you at your clinic the same day."

"Glad to hear it. Thanks for making that happen. When I learned that the Huancayo clinic hadn't been open for over a year, I knew we should get a surgeon up there if at all possible. So I appreciate you going." And never mind that lack of recent care wasn't the only reason he'd wanted to get it open for business.

"We Peruvians have to look after our own when we can, right? Alan and I'll be at your clinic on Tuesday with a nurse who's agreed to help me, then I'll take the anesthesiologist you want working with me down to Huancayo."

Peruvians looked after their own? He knew that wasn't always true. Those like his own family with education and wealth and privilege were certainly well taken care of. But those living in poverty on the other side of the infamous wall of shame in Lima that had been compared to the Berlin Wall? The deeply poor living in the many remote towns in Peru that the various mission groups were devoted to help? Not so much.

"Thanks again. I'll let Dr. Richards know she'll be helping get the clinic open in Huancayo. See you when you get here."

He should be elated, since this was exactly how he'd hoped it would all turn out. Instead, a small knot formed in his gut as he pondered how to talk to Annabelle about the change of plans. But surely, if he played it right, she'd be happy to be helping patients in a part of the country that hadn't received medical care or surgeries for a long time. Right?

Daniel shook off his unease and headed back

toward the hotel. Whatever he was feeling was ridiculous and made no sense. He'd have a top-notch anesthesiologist working with him on the delicate heart surgeries, and more children and adults with health problems would be seen during the next couple of weeks in Huancayo, where the need was real. Annabelle might never know he'd been the one to get the clinic open but even if she did, she'd probably assume it had come about organically, without any agenda other than having more doctors available to care for more patients. A win for everyone.

The shining halo of Annabelle's pale blond hair shone through the falling darkness in front of the hotel, just as it had at dawn this morning, spilling to her shoulders in silky waves. His steps slowed as he thought through how he was going to tell her about the change of plans in a way that would make her feel fine about it. Then stopped completely to watch her crouch down to a feral cat, offering it a morsel of food that had it purring and rubbing against her ankles. The sexy roundness of her bottom and hips caught his attention, and the sweet, low sound of her voice crept under his skin.

"Ah, you're such a little sweetie, aren't you?" she cooed, her voice dropping to a whisper. "The hotel manager told me not to feed you, so this is just between us, okay? No more meowing out here in the middle of the night. Got it?"

In answer, the cat flopped onto its back, purring even louder, and Annabelle laughed softly as she scratched its belly, an indulgent smile on her face. "I can tell you're going to get me in trouble. Just so you know, I'm going to swear it wasn't me giving you treats. We'll blame Daniel Ferrera instead, but you have to back me up on this."

"Won't work," Daniel said, a smile twitching his lips even as he wanted to ask her why she'd put the blame on him instead of someone else staying in the hotel. "I'm now a witness to your illicit activities."

Annabelle jumped to her feet, twisting to face him, and her alarmed and guilty expression nearly made him chuckle. "Oh! Dr. Ferrera. Why are you sneaking up on people in the dark like that? You startled me."

"My apologies. I didn't realize it could be considered sneaking since I was walking in full view on the designated path to the front door."

"Well, it's almost dark and you should have made more noise."

"So I wouldn't hear you plotting against me?"

She folded her arms across her chest and stared him down. "If I did plot against you, it would be tit for tat, wouldn't it? However, I'm not that kind of person."

"Uh-huh. No way am I going to be the fall guy if a cacophony of meows wakes up the whole hotel."

"I was just kidding about blaming you. Even though you blamed me for something that wasn't my fault. Or at least was only partially my fault. But that's long over with and I'm going to put it behind me. No plotting against you."

That knocked the smile off his face because, yeah, it wouldn't be a stretch to say he was plotting against her, given everything he'd orchestrated to get her services transferred to the other clinic.

"Anyway," she continued in a stiff and professional voice that had him regretting that their light banter was obviously over, "what's tomorrow's surgical schedule?"

"Full day again," he replied. "We need to get going no later than seven to fit them all in, especially since a couple of the diagnostics we were given aren't very clear. May find some surprises during surgery that will take longer than we expect."

"That happens about fifty percent of the time anyway," she said as she slung the small green backpack over her shoulder that she seemed to carry everywhere.

"True." Now was the time to tell her about the new plans for her upcoming trip to Huancayo, and he hoped she was perfectly fine with it, not figuring there was anything to it other than helping more people. He drew a breath, only to expel it as he watched her move the backpack strap down to the crook of her elbow, her face scrunching up a little with obvious discomfort as she reached to massage her neck and shoulder. "Is your arm hurting you?"

"I don't want to say." Her voice was mulish even as she winced. "Especially to you."

"Why not?"

"What procedure does our first patient need?" she asked, ignoring his question and dropping her hand from her trapezius muscle. "I want to be ready with everything so we stay on schedule and maybe even catch up a little."

"Four-year-old has coarctation of the aorta, but I suspect we may find more issues during surgery, as the imaging isn't very good. Tell me why your arm hurts."

"I took a swing at an arrogant, holier-than-thou doctor in the States just before leaving there. Very satisfying, but I miscalculated the impact on my own body."

"Uh-huh. I know you wanted to take a swing at me five years ago, maybe even with a long, sharp knife. But since you didn't, violence doesn't seem to be your answer to conflict." He reached to fold her hand into a fist and tapped it against his chin. "However, if you want to punch me now and get it out of your system, go ahead. I can take it."

A short laugh, then a scowl, before she yanked her hand back. "No, thanks. That would probably just make you happy in some perverse kind of way, and give you another reason to dislike me or get me fired again. Forget it."

"Then tell me about your shoulder." He stepped closer and could smell the faint scent of soap from her shower before dinner. "Or let me guess. You don't want to tell me that you're in pain because you wrenched it carrying the monitor I criticized you for."

Surprised blue eyes lifted to his, her pretty lips parting. "I knew you had superpowers in the operating room, but it's scary to think you have mind reading powers, too."

"Simple observation and medical skills. But if I did have mind-reading abilities, what would I be learning?"

"That I don't like you?"

"Something I already know. What else?"

A long pause had him convinced she'd change the subject, or turn and walk back into the hotel, until she finally spoke on a sigh. "That I sometimes bite off more than I can chew, and hate it so much when I do." A deep frown lowered over her silky eyebrows. "And I've paid for this one multiple times, believe me. First with stressing over all the missed flights, then with not being able to get to a meeting in Lima that I really need to make happen. And I'm still not sure how I'm going to be able to get it rescheduled. Then missing the first day of surgery, which I worried about a lot, even though you probably don't believe that. On top of that, yeah, I wrenched my shoulder trying to carry the monitor to the OR in a hurry. And the worst thing of all? Letting it show so you can smirk at me about it."

"I would never smirk at you or anyone else who's in pain. I'm a doctor, for heaven's sake." While he knew all the reasons she didn't like him, he hadn't realized she thought he was the kind of colossal jerk who would delight in some-one's pain. "Come here and let me see."

"What?" She jerked back as he stepped close. "No."

"You can't function as well in the OR if your shoulder is stiff and painful. And since it's im-portant for everyone to be at peak performance during surgeries that last for hours, I'm going to give you a deep-tissue massage that should help."

"I don't want or need a massage." Her expres-sion was more alarmed than a simple shoulder massage should have warranted, displaying a vulnerability at odds with her stern words. "It's fine. Really. And frankly it's a bad idea for col-leagues to go around touching one another, es-pecially when anyone could be watching."

"Anyone watching would see it as impersonal physiotherapy done in a very public place, right outside the hotel front door. Are you always so stubborn? Or are you worried that I'm coming on to you? I know that probably happens a lot but, believe me, I have no interest in you other than that you do your best tomorrow during the long hours we have to work."

"An interest in me other than to ruin my career would never cross my mind, Dr. Ferrera. And the feeling is mutual."

"Good. So quit arguing and turn around."

CHAPTER THREE

WHY SHE ALLOWED him to turn her around, then press his fingers deeply into her shoulder muscles, Annabelle had no idea. But even as she told herself it was weird to do this, that she should just turn to head for the hotel doors and disappear to her room before the man started criticizing her again, she found herself standing stock still instead as she absorbed the feel of his hands.

Lord have mercy. Was this why people spent their hard-earned money to get a massage? She couldn't believe how incredibly good it felt, as though his palms and fingers were magical instruments, kneading and pressing until the tightly knotted muscles began to loosen. His warm breath skimmed her neck as he worked, and it all felt so wonderful, every other thought in her head disappeared, and all worries along with it. Slowly tipping her head from one side to the other, she nearly moaned with the pleasure of those talented surgeon's hands firmly moving on her neck and over her shoulders, working their way down to press against her spine.

"Take a deep breath, then blow it out. Then again."

She obeyed, her eyelids fluttering closed at the sensations, even as a tiny part of her mind managed to ask why she was allowing annoying Daniel Ferrera to give her this amazing massage, professional and impersonal or not.

"Good?" he asked, his voice a low murmur in her ear.

"Mmm… Yes. Good." That breathy word didn't begin to cover it, but her brain wasn't functioning well enough to come up with something else. His cheek almost brushed hers, so close she could practically feel the warmth of it radiating against her skin. Each time she drew breath his delicious scent filled her nose. Just as she was sinking so deeply into the sensory overload that she nearly forgot where she was, he abruptly removed his hands and stepped back.

Nearly swaying at the suddenness of it, she blinked and slowly turned toward him, surprised to see he looked oddly grim instead of satisfied that he'd helped the knots unkink. "Um, thank you. That did help a lot, I have to admit."

"Good." He ran that wide hand of his through his hair as he seemed to concentrate on something over her head. She glanced over her shoulder, and when she saw nothing there, turned back to see Daniel, now standing with his hands in his pockets, staring at her. "Listen. I want to talk to you about the phone call I got a little while ago."

Something about his tone set an alarm clanging in her head, though she couldn't say exactly why. "What call?"

"There's a clinic near Huancayo that hasn't been staffed and ready to see patients in over a year. A surgeon friend of mine wants to open it while we're here so he can do things like hernia and gallbladder surgeries that are urgently needed by people in the area. He needs an anesthesiologist. I told him you'd probably be fine with going there."

"I don't understand. You can't do surgeries here without me."

"Alan Velasco, an anesthesiologist friend from Lima that I've worked with a number of times before, is going to come here to take your place. So we'll be able to take care of a lot more patients than we'd originally thought, with both clinics open. Which is good news."

Cool and impassive was the only way to describe his expression, and there was something peculiar about it. Something that didn't quite fit with this new opportunity. "When would this happen?"

"Alan said that he and the surgeon, Eduardo Diaz, could be here the day after tomorrow. So, soon."

Her heart lurched as she pondered how that could possibly work. She absolutely had to get the meeting she'd missed in Lima rescheduled before she went back home. Before the school she wanted to save closed for good and got knocked down by a wrecking ball, which would happen in just two months if she couldn't pull her plan together in time.

What if the doctor and CEO at the hospital in Lima who were interested in partnering with her wanted her to be there a specific evening after work to hear the details? She needed to be close enough to go running if they found time to squeeze her into their schedules.

About to ask more questions and explain why going to Huancayo might not work for her, she paused to study him. Really looked at his chiseled jaw and handsome features, the deep brown of his eyes that she'd thought were beautiful and mesmerizing when she'd first met him in Philadelphia long ago. Every woman in that hospital had swooned over Dr. Daniel Ferrera. And, yeah, she'd secretly been one of them until she'd learned his amazing attractiveness on the outside was the polar opposite of his personality.

Reading people and their body language, carefully listening to verbal cues and paying attention to their eyes, their expressions, had been an essential survival skill for Annabelle growing up. Studying him now, her antennae went on red alert, telling her something was really off here. She let herself absorb it, think through whatever subtext there might be between the lines of his actual words.

Then the *Aha!* came like a sledgehammer to her chest. The shock of it, along with the intense burn filling her gut and the heat scorching her head, finally had her seeing right through the jerk.

"You arranged this, didn't you? You hate working with me so much that you've arranged for me to go to the other clinic so you could work with this Alan guy."

"I don't hate working with you. I simply saw this as an opportunity to have more patients get the surgeries they need."

"That is such bull! I'm not stupid, Dr. Ferrera, even though you clearly have always thought I am. You worked all this out, no doubt smug as hell as you did it, convincing yourself it was perfectly fine and somehow win-win because more patients will be seen, no matter how wrong your motivation is."

"It is a win-win. Alan has a lot of experience with heart surgeries, and you'll be helping people who need medical procedures and advice near Huancayo. That's it."

"That is so not *it*. Do you spend your life manipulating everyone and everything around you? Always able to convince yourself you're doing it for your patients, instead of out of some nasty need for complete control?" Shaking now from the top of her head to the soles of her feet, Annabelle jabbed him hard in the sternum, wanting so much to punch him instead, just as he'd offered to let her do earlier. The only time she could remember being this upset and furious had been the last time Daniel had screwed her over.

"You stink as a human being, you know that? You really do. I'm contacting the mission heads about this. If they go along with what you want, which everyone seems to do, I'll work in Huancayo. But I'm telling you right now that I may have to leave there to get to an extremely important meeting in Lima, which is a lot longer drive from there than from here. Once I have it scheduled, I have to get there, and I don't care how you feel about that. I'd rather not leave the clinic without an anesthesiologist, but you're the one creating this situation."

"Is this much drama really warranted, Dr. Richards? I'd think you'd be glad to not work with me. Less stress for you in the OR," he drawled. "I'm not creating a situation. I'm getting a clinic open to serve more patients. I thought you'd be as pleased about that as I am."

"Seeing more patients is always good. But there's an agenda attached to that, and it has to do with me," she said between her teeth. "Just so you know, when I contact the mission management, I'm telling them about how you think your surgeon status makes you godlike. But you know what?" Lord, she hated that her voice quivered, making her sound weak. "You're not a god. You're not, no matter how much you want to play like you are."

"I have no illusions of being a god. If I was,

my life would be different, believe me." All cool relaxation left his voice, the harsh planes of his face looking etched from stone. "Maybe it's past time for you to see that none of this is about you, and never has been. It's always been about the patients facing death. Facing pain and suffering and lifelong complications. About the people who love them and who are devastated when a surgery goes wrong, or a condition is left untreated. About those left behind having to pick up the pieces of their lives. It always has been, and always will be, and I have to believe you care about them as much as I do.

"I'll see you in the OR in the morning. Maybe you can get your meeting in Lima scheduled for tomorrow night. Then get your stuff ready so you can go to Huancayo with Dr. Eduardo Diaz when he gets here the day after."

He swiveled toward the hotel, and Annabelle watched the back of his tall, broad form as he walked, his shoulders stiff, his posture proud. Watched the heavy hotel doors close, leaving behind the smothering cloud of disapproval. Of pity for who she was and convictions about who she could never be. It rolled over her, consumed her, until she couldn't breathe.

Blindly, she stumbled to the pathway into the woods beside the hotel, sucking in air.

We heard you're homeless again, Annabelle. Can you tell us how many different schools you've attended this year?

Let's see what clothes are in the office storage closet, Annabelle. We'll just throw away the ones you're wearing.

Go to college? That's just silly, Annabelle. You need to set realistic goals.

She smacked her palms against the rough bark of a wide tree. Rested her forehead against it and gulped air, welcoming the painful prickling against her forehead.

Only one person in her life had believed in her back then. One special high school guidance counselor who had seen past her dirty clothes and face. Noticed how focused she'd been on her studies, how she'd got good grades despite being yanked in and out of different schools every time her mother's drug- and alcohol-fueled life had got messy, which had been most of the time. She'd learned early that the only way she would survive the hunger, the bad living conditions, being utterly alone when her mother left for weeks on a bender, was to be smarter, work harder than everyone else around her. To read and to dream.

That special counselor had introduced her to a group promoting medicine as a career path for high schoolers to consider. The instant she'd walked into that hospital, met doctors and nurses and technicians, had seen the amazing equipment and felt the busy, pulsing rhythm of the place as it treated people and saved lives, she'd known that becoming a doctor was all she wanted to do.

Everyone had constantly tried to send her in a different direction, warning her it wouldn't be easy. And it wasn't. But nothing ever had been. Working two jobs while going to college, then medical school, had been the best years of her life. For the first time, she'd believed all the dreams she'd had over the years could really come true. Had seen her path and run without stopping. Applied for every scholarship she could dig up. Worked hard to get the kinds of grades that added academic scholarships to the needs-based ones. Once she'd finished medical school and moved on to her training residency in Philadelphia, she'd been blessed with the mentorship and support of a few special doctors and administrators there. Wonderful people who'd found extra grant money for her to survive.

Her tough times were history. Behind her. Not who she was now, and not who she'd ever be again.

Except that wasn't true, was it? A part of her would always be that poor little girl with filthy clothes and dirt on her skin being judged by everyone around her. Being found lacking, pathetic, incapable, no matter how hard she worked to try to prove she could be more than that.

For long moments she let herself wallow in the painful memories. The terrible, negative feelings. The ridicule and doubt. Remember the past that still clung to her shoes, no matter how hard she stomped her feet, or how fast she ran to knock off every embarrassing and ugly thing that proved her status as a misfit. And she prayed that, on top of everything else, Daniel would never know where she'd come from, and who she really was.

She drew in long, deep breaths. In and out. In and out. Using the meditation techniques that had helped her move into a world completely different from the one she'd grown up in. To find the steely determination she'd had to call on her whole life, her resolution that she'd go from being on the lowest rungs of society to someone who helped those still there. After long minutes she stiffened her spine and stood tall.

Dr. Daniel Ferrera was just a nasty bump from her past that she'd had the misfortune to run into again. But she wouldn't allow him to hurt her, or make her think less of herself. Wouldn't let him or anyone else make her forget why she was here. Wouldn't waste another moment thinking about a man who chewed people up and spit them out with the excuse that he was doing it for a good reason.

She had important things to accomplish here,

and one of the biggest was getting the hospital school meeting set up. She would do whatever it took to convince them of why they should partner with the Chicago hospital where she worked, and save the school, turning it into a charter school that offered medical career path options to poor, disadvantaged high school kids like she'd been, changing lives for the better in the process. The way her own life had been changed.

Once that was done she'd go to Huancayo and do the best she could there. Focus on the chance to help children and adults with problems that made it harder for them to live comfortably and happily.

It didn't take a heart surgeon to make a difference in people's lives. It just took someone with heart, and that was at least one thing she knew for certain she had enough of.

As much as Daniel tried to keep his interactions with Annabelle completely normal during surgery the next morning and throughout the day, the strain between them hung in the room like a thick cloud.

He'd always prided himself on being tough but fair. But something about Annabelle seemed to bring out an extreme version of his stern and unyielding side. The scowls she'd sent on and off all day made him start to hear it and see it in himself, and he knew that was something he had to fix.

Ultimately, the only thing that mattered was delivering the best care they could all give to each and every patient. Not anyone's fragile feelings. After all, delicate surgeries weren't a popularity contest or touchy-feely bonding with medical friends, they were about results.

But part of good patient care was having a cohesive team that worked well together. Something he'd allowed himself to forget when he'd first seen her here, letting his distrust of her overflow into the OR. Five years ago she'd earned his conviction that she shouldn't be working on these kinds of surgeries, and he stood by what he'd said and done back then. But her work here had been good so far, and he should probably tell her that. Maybe it would make everyone on the team feel less stress in the OR.

One glance at her tight lips and stony expression as she removed the IV lines from their patient told him that fixing, at least a little, the rift between them wasn't going to be easy. Maybe it was just too late, pointless even, since they wouldn't be working together much longer.

Daniel drew in a deep breath and shoved away those questions to focus on the patient, checking to make sure all his vital signs were where they should be post-op. "He looks good. Nice job, everyone." He pulled off his gloves and scrub cap, then rolled his head to relieve the tense kinks after hours of being mostly stationary during surgery, pausing briefly to look at Annabelle out of the corner of his eye as he did. He watched her face soften as she talked to the child and stroked his cheek, helping him awaken, and had to admit to himself again how wonderful her bedside manner was. Something not true of every anesthesiologist. "After he's in Recovery, we'll stretch our legs and break for dinner. Then I'd like to get one more in tonight."

"I'm all for that," Jennifer said as she cleaned the instruments. "I need a serious bellyful of food first, though. Who'll be the last patient?"

"A little girl with patent ductus arteriosus," he replied. "I thought about moving her down the list, maybe seeing her next time because she's doing all right at the moment, but I figured since it's going to be a comparatively easy and short surgery we can fit her in for the ligation tonight. What do you say we eat, then get back here in an hour so we can all get a decent night's sleep afterwards?"

"No arguments from me," Karina said.

He noticed Karina and Jennifer glanced at Annabelle, both looking a little concerned. Probably wondering if she'd eat with them, since she'd declined to join them at lunch. Maybe they knew as well as he did that it was because she didn't want to make small talk with him. Since he didn't particularly want to do that either, he wondered why it had bothered him that she'd eaten alone.

Annabelle didn't say a word on their trek along the scrubby, rock-strewn path back to the hotel, even though the nurses chatted nonstop. The conversation sounded a little forced, and he had a feeling they were trying to make up for the discomfort hovering in the air.

Daniel couldn't seem to keep his eyes off Annabelle, noting the way the hair tucked behind her ears was starting to curl, as it always seemed to do around this time of day once she took off her scrub cap. Even this late in the day, the temperature was still in the mideighties, which might be why he was sweating. Or maybe it was because he was trying to figure out what to say to her.

Except her attention seemed utterly focused on the path ahead of them. A focus so intense he couldn't imagine how she managed to stumble over a stone, but he saw her toe catch just before she plunged headlong toward the rocky path.

His heart gave a jolt and he leaped toward her, shooting out his arm to grab her before she ended up falling flat and hurting herself. His other arm instinctively wrapped around her back as he yanked her upright, pulling her hard against his chest. The feel of her full, soft breasts pressing against him somehow had him folding her even closer as her startled eyes looked up into his. The moment lasted long, breathless seconds and he realized he didn't want to move.

Her eyes seemed to reflect the same uncertainty he felt until she pulled herself free, nearly stumbling again in her haste to step away. The confusion he'd seen in her gaze morphed into an icy stare that seemed to instantly cool the temperature down about ten degrees. It was the kind of expression that the term *if looks could kill* was based on.

"You okay?"

"Fine. Thanks." She took a few more steps away. "Listen, I kind of want to be alone for a while," she said, directing her comment to Jennifer and Karina. "I'm going to grab some food from the hotel and eat by myself again. See you all back in the OR."

He watched her hips sway as she hurried ahead

of them; how she somehow made scrubs look almost sexy, he didn't know. Feeling relieved that he wouldn't have to figure out how to make small talk with her, or endure being shut out and ignored throughout dinner, he realized that, at the same time, disappointment filled his chest that she wouldn't be at the table with them. Which made zero sense, and he disgustedly shook it off. He'd just have to make time later tonight to talk with her alone and try to clear the air.

"Is something bothering Annabelle?" Karina asked in a low voice.

"Not sure." Jennifer glanced up at Daniel, and it was pretty clear she knew exactly what was bothering Annabelle. "I think she might be unhappy that the shipment of equipment hasn't made it here yet."

"What shipment?" Daniel asked, wondering if there really could be a reason she was unhappy besides her anger at him.

"She has that Med Mission Wishes nonprofit she set up a few years ago, you know? She's been collecting the newest batch at her hospital for about three months, but for some reason what she wanted sent here hasn't shown up yet."

"Med Mission what?"

"Wishes. It might be available where you work, since she's grown it so much. Bins are set up in hospitals for people to save all the stuff that would normally be thrown away but which can be used in places like this."

"Such as?"

"Things like tubing and new syringes, airway stuff, outdated surgical tools, all kinds of things. You know how much is thrown out at home, even if it's brand new and the hospital just has a new vendor or something." Jennifer gave him a look that said he should know all about this nonprofit. "So she started the organization, and after a while it grew so much she pays someone to run it now. To get it collected and inventoried and warehoused in a building in Chicago. Then medical missions from all over the world buy it by the pound."

"Ah, I remember you were about to say something about this before, but for some reason Annabelle didn't want you to."

"Usually she wants to tell everyone, to get them involved." Jennifer gave him a pointed look that said she knew all about the issues between the two of them.

"She's the one who started it?" He wanted to be clear on that, since he just might have to talk with her about it. It was a smart thing to be doing, and they definitely needed to bring it to his hospital in Philadelphia.

"Yeah, she was appalled by the waste when we barely have the minimum of what we need to make these clinics run. Their website shows all the places in the world where Med Mission Wishes materials are used now. I admire her so much, especially considering where she came from. I don't know a single person working at these medical missions who cares more about the people we serve here. And about all the folks coming to the Chicago free clinics, too."

"What do you mean, where she came from? Isn't she from Chicago?"

"Um, yeah. She is." Jennifer's expression was suddenly cautious. "Anyway, hopefully the box of stuff will come soon. But if it doesn't, we'll have to get by with what she already brought. So, how about that dinner? I'm starved."

Something about the abrupt way she changed the subject made him wonder why she had. Did Annabelle have secrets about her life that she didn't want Jennifer to share?

"Me, too. Let's go," Karina said.

Suddenly, Daniel didn't particularly want to eat dinner and make small talk with Jen and Karina any more than Annabelle had. Not when he should take this opportunity to talk with her about his realization that he'd perhaps been tougher on her than he'd needed to be. He wasn't going to apologize for greasing the wheels for her to go to Huancayo, because he still felt that was a good plan all around.

But he would tell the woman she'd done a good job in the OR the past couple of days, and that he was also impressed with her vision and work on collecting equipment in the United States for these missions. He found himself eager to find out what he needed to do to have his own hospital participate.

"I'm going to find Dr. Richards to make sure she's okay, and grab something to eat after I talk to her."

Both women looked at him a little quizzically as they nodded and moved into the small hotel dining room. Probably they'd be gossiping about him and Annabelle and wondering if they'd make up or not.

Daniel moved up the path from the hotel through the trees to find Annabelle. Or at least he assumed she'd be somewhere along there, as it was the only path the goats had trekked enough to make it decent to walk on, with the rest of the hills covered in scrub brush and stones or steep, rocky inclines.

Just as he was wondering if maybe she'd somehow taken another route, he saw her sitting on the ground with her back against a tree, and paused. Her blond head was tipped downward, her hair skimming her cheeks. She took a last bite of whatever she'd been eating then brushed her hands down her chest then across her lap. His gaze became fixated on the slow movement of her hands moving down her chest a second time, molding the curves beneath her scrub shirt, nearly cupping her breasts, and a surprising flood of heat filled Daniel's body as he pictured his own hands replacing hers.

No, not surprising. He and Annabelle might have their differences, but she was a beautiful woman and he was a warm-blooded man. Of course he found it impossible to not think about how she'd felt in his arms when he'd caught her earlier, those lush curves pressed against his body. To wonder what it would be like to kiss her lips, so soft-looking now compared to how they usually looked when she spoke to him— compressed and irritated.

He found himself wanting to just stand there and watch her, because he knew that all that softness would disappear as soon as she saw him. But he'd come to talk to her about their conflicts and her nonprofit equipment collection, and he needed to make that happen while he had the chance.

His movement toward her must have caught her attention, as she lifted her gaze to his. Sure enough, her pretty lips pinched together and her gorgeous eyes narrowed. As far as she was concerned, he was obviously the enemy, and he didn't know if there was a way to fix that, considering everything. But he had to try, to make the whole team more comfortable in the OR during the time she was still here.

"Before you go off on me, I have a couple things I want to talk to you about," he said, lifting his palm to stop whatever angry comment she was clearly ready to fling his way.

"What this time? Have you convinced the mission heads that I'm too incompetent to even work at the other clinic? Thrown your weight around the way you did in Philadelphia? Made a plane reservation for me to go back to the States right this minute, dragging a bad reputation home with me?"

"No, I want to talk to you about your good reputation."

She folded her arms across her chest and glared. "Yeah, right. This isn't a cold day in hell, you know."

In spite of everything, his lips quirked at what a spitfire she was. "Doesn't need to be a cold day in hell for me to tell you that you've done a good job here so far, and that I know you'll do fine work at the clinic in Huancayo."

A suspicious stare was her only response, and he forged on, hoping they could at least make a little progress toward having a better working relationship.

"And Jennifer just told me about your Med Mission Wishes organization. It's a good thing, a valuable thing, and I should have thought of it myself. But since I didn't, I'd like to find out how I can bring it to my hospital, too."

"You're not finding a reason to criticize me for it?" Her eyebrows rose in clear surprise, and there was no mistaking the skeptical look she sent him. "You want your hospital to participate?"

"Of course I wouldn't criticize you for it. How could I, when it's a brilliant idea? And you know the size of the hospital where I work, the amount of equipment we'd be able to donate."

He dropped down onto the dirt and soft plants surrounding the tree to sit next to her. Because his back was tired from standing all day he let himself lean back against it, nearly shoulder to shoulder with her. It felt oddly comfortable, and he was glad she didn't scoot away. "I want to get your bins set up there, learn about the distribution and where all it goes around the world. How to ensure some of it gets sent here, to the various clinics in Peru."

"Having your hospital in the loop would be good. I already know you have an obnoxious amount of clout there and think everyone should do your bidding. But in this case it would be helpful." She tipped her head and seemed to study him, and he found himself mesmerized by the little flecks of green and gold inside the beautiful blue of her eyes.

For what seemed like long seconds they just

looked at one another. Apparently, she finally decided he was completely sincere, since the suspicious frown vanished. "All right. After I get home, I'll send you all the information about how to sign up and how it works, and hopefully the hospital administrators will agree."

"I'll make it happen."

"Always the autocrat." She rolled her eyes. "But just this once I appreciate that about you. It's a deal, though you or someone else from the hospital will have to earmark some of it for Peruvian clinics, as that's done at the local level."

"I'll take care of that. Thank you."

"You thanking me for something," she murmured, looking up at him as though she genuinely found it incomprehensible. "Now, there's a shock."

"I've thanked you in the OR. I know I have. You only hear the negative when it's me speaking."

"Maybe. And with good reason."

"Annabelle." He found himself reaching for her soft hand without thinking, and was surprised she let it stay in his grasp. "I want us to have a good working relationship. Mutual respect is important to a smoothly operating OR, and even though it might irritate you to hear me say it again, a cohesive team is important for surgeries to go as well as possible."

"I agree. The problem is, you don't respect me."

Along with the flash of frustration and indignation in her eyes, was he seeing something like self-doubt? In every one of their interactions, five years ago and here, she'd come out fighting for herself. Was it bravado, hiding some kind of insecurity? Was she not as confident as she seemed?

"I do respect you." He leaned closer, wanting her to really hear him. "Today I realized that I haven't given you the praise you deserve. I've seen that you're good at your job and great with patients. It's just that I need to know with one hundred percent certainty that everyone on a team doing open-heart surgeries is the absolute best. Surely you can understand that, after what happened before, I—"

His phone jangled in his pocket, and he nearly

didn't answer it, wanting to finish this conversation. Impatient, he fished it out and saw a number he didn't recognize.

"Daniel Ferrera."

"Dr. Ferrera, it's Luciana, at the Huancayo clinic. I'm here getting it cleaned up and ready to open. A little while ago I was surprised when a family banged on the door. They heard we were opening and were worried about their eight-month-old. He's been in respiratory distress, wheezing. Hasn't been eating well. They thought he had a bad cold and might need some medication. So I listened to the baby's chest, and I'm positive he's in congestive heart failure. Luckily, we still have an old echocardiogram machine here, and it showed deep and wide waves. Seems to be ALCAPA."

"Damn." If Luciana was right, there was a real risk of sudden cardiac death for the child. "I need to get there. We'll leave as soon as possible, but it's at least a three-hour drive. I'll bring the anesthesiologist we have here. You have the equipment we need?"

"No. There's nothing here right now."

"I'll see what we have that we can bring. Expect us no later than eleven, and be ready to assist."

"Got it."

"We need to get to Huancayo tonight?" Annabelle's question was asked in a matter-of-fact tone. Her angry expression and clear frustration with him was gone, replaced by a calm professionalism, and he had to give her credit for that. For putting work and patients before the emotions that kept flaring up between them.

"Yes." They both started moving down the path toward the hotel. "The nurse opening the clinic said there's a baby that needs surgery as soon as possible. We'll have to take the equipment from here. I'll do an inventory of what we have, to see if we have any extra that I can leave there."

"Already done. I took a full inventory the first day I got here, including what I'd brought with me."

"Good." He felt a stab of shame at his ongoing doubts about her not being quite good enough at her job for him to feel confident in her. Noting all the equipment available was something usually done by nurses, not the anesthesiologist, not to mention she'd had the foresight to bring more. Then again, being organized in that way was a totally different thing than delivering anesthesia to the sickest patients during long and serious surgeries. "That will save us time, but I can't imagine it's enough for both places, is it?"

"Probably not. If only the stuff I shipped had gotten here already."

"Yeah, that's unfortunate. But from what you've said, it should be here soon, right? So it'll be good to have on hand here after we get back. With more equipment coming, we can leave whatever we take to Huancayo. And I'll see what Eduardo can provide when he gets there." He stopped at the fork in the path. "Let's start at the OR, getting stuff together, before we pack and take off."

He shoved open the OR door and snapped on the lights. Annabelle quickly began pulling together the necessary anesthesia items as he gathered the surgical ones.

"Dare I suggest we take the monitor, or will you have another fit about it?" Annabelle asked.

"I don't have fits. You make me sound childish."

"Well, you know the saying, if the shoe fits…"

The little smirk she sent him took any sting from the words and he couldn't help but grin back. "A part of me doesn't want to see you gloat, but the *mature* part of me says to take the monitor. If it's really ALCAPA, it'll be a long, tricky surgery."

"Acknowledgement that it's handy to have is all I wanted to hear, Dr. Ferrera."

It was on the tip of his tongue to say she still should have shipped it instead of being so late because of it, but hadn't he decided to stop being so rigid and critical with her? So he kept his mouth shut and concentrated on making sure he had all the surgical supplies he'd need. He and Annabelle packed things so efficiently together he couldn't help but think they were like a well-oiled machine, and neither interrupted their work even when the door swung open again.

"You guys are back fast," Jennifer said, walking in with a big box in her arms. "Good news! Your package came, Annabelle. I'll go through it tomorrow to see what all's in here."

"Can you do it now? We have an emergency surgery in Huancayo, and it would help to see what we can leave up there."

"No problem. What should I tell the little girl and her family who were expecting her to get treatment tonight?" Jennifer asked.

Before Daniel could say anything Annabelle briskly and efficiently went through her mental roster of the next morning's surgeries and suggested the best way to fit the young patient in. He couldn't blame her for the look of triumph there, the slow curving of her mouth. "See, Dr. Ferrera? I'm not worthless at all. Maybe you'll actually come to appreciate me."

"Never said you were worthless, and as for appreciating you? It might surprise you to hear that just might be happening already."

CHAPTER FOUR

"THE CLINIC IS right around this next curve," Daniel said, turning to Annabelle with a slightly tired smile. "I think we made good time."

"Probably because you drove like a maniac. It's a wonder I didn't have a heart attack and need a cardiologist. Good thing there was one close by."

A soft laugh left his lips, his eyes gleaming at her through the dark interior of the car, and she found herself staring at how much younger and more handsome he looked when he was relaxed and away from the OR. At least for the moment.

"I'd have let you drive except for that whole controlling streak of mine you've already noted."

"And I'd have declined anyway, since I'm sure you're the worst backseat driver in the whole world."

Again, he laughed, and she had to quickly turn

away from the unexpected charm of his smile. The same way she had the past three hours of semi-torture, sitting way too closely to the man who utterly confused her. One minute he was being a total jerk toward her, then the next he was sitting snugged up next to her against that tree and holding her hand in his large grasp. Sending a smile her way that was so sexy and attractive she'd nearly forgotten how much she disliked him.

All through the drive it had been a huge effort to not frequently glance over at his handsome profile. At his firm jaw and nicely shaped mouth. To not think far too much about how large and masculine he was. To not make too big a deal out of the seemingly sincere admiration in his warm, dark eyes as he'd looked at her beneath that tree and told her she was doing a good job and that he respected her.

Because, yeah, he'd then quickly followed that praise with a statement about needing the best anesthesiologist for difficult heart surgeries, and he clearly still didn't believe she was that person.

The friendly banter on this car ride, completely different from the friction in all their exchanges before this, had thrown her off guard, making her see him in a way she didn't want to. Her completely unexpected and unwelcome feelings of attraction to the man were a whole lot of stupid for a whole lot of reasons, and she wouldn't let herself think about his sex appeal for one more second.

The car growled to a stop, and she was more than glad to have something else to focus on in the darkness of the night, when his shadowed shape next to her had been the only thing she'd been able to see and think about, the scent of him filling her nose the way it had earlier that evening.

She peered at the building in front of them, very similar to the one in Ayllu that she'd always worked in on her trips to Peru. The one she'd never dreamed Daniel Ferrera would end up working in, too. This one, though, looked a little more worn and neglected. Faded green paint peeled from the cement walls, exposed by a single, dangling bulb of light above the front step. Scrubby plants and weeds grew all around its perimeter, and the door was slightly off-kilter on its hinges.

"Looks like the front door doesn't really close," she said. "Not a good thing when it comes to keeping the space as sterile as possible."

"Not a good thing for keeping creatures out either." Another one of those smiles that made her ridiculous heart inexplicably flutter.

"Very true." She reached for her seat belt, more than happy to get out of the car and away from the close proximity to Daniel. "I'd been congratulating your home country at the miles and miles of completely paved roads we drove on to get to Huancayo. Then we hit that last however many miles of dirt and rocks outside the city to get up here, and I'm pretty sure it might have jarred one of my teeth loose."

"Don't worry. I could probably perform emergency oral surgery if I absolutely had to."

That startled a laugh out of her. "Thanks, but, no, thanks. I'd eat through a straw for the rest of my life before I'd submit to something so terrifying."

"Smart woman." Daniel sent her another quick grin before he pulled the monitor and oxygen tank from the back of the car, and it struck her that the past hours had been the first time she'd seen a smile on his face quite like that. Laidback and friendly and genuinely amused. "Not to mention that we have a different kind of surgery to get to ASAP. Luciana said the child is inside, prepped and ready to go, so let's get to it."

Grabbing the rest of the items they'd brought for the surgery, including the cooler of blood bags, Annabelle followed him. She was determined to keep the conversation either light, like the tooth comment, professional, talking about how they would approach diagnosing the child's problem to ensure they got it right, or nonexistent. Keeping somewhat of a distance between them and forgetting all about her sudden, peculiar attraction to the man.

His good looks couldn't erase their former animosity, and certainly didn't replace his ongoing doubts about her skills. Sure, he'd said he was finally coming to respect her more, but it had been too little too late, as far as she was concerned.

No, she'd shake off whatever it was that was making her feel so weird and just be glad they were forming a better working relationship. Because taking the best care of patients they possibly could was their whole purpose for being here.

Once inside the door, Annabelle tried to adjust her eyes to the space, lit just slightly by a small table lamp. Obviously, it was a small entryway that probably served as the greeting room for patients and families, the way the bigger space at the other clinic did. A wooden desk sat in front of a row of folding chairs, and the room had an antiseptic soap smell to it.

"Luciana's obviously been at work cleaning this place up, probably with the help of locals. Last time I came, I was with the first crew to arrive and it was quite a battle to sweep out all the cobwebs and dust, along with a nest of baby opossums and their mother, who was not happy to have her family disturbed."

"Is that what you meant by creatures coming in? Good heavens. Where were they?" That the man had actually helped clean this place and chase out marsupials was a surprise. She'd always viewed him as a guy who thought of himself as the holier-than-thou king of the OR, and not someone who would pitch in with that kind of grunt work.

"In a mostly empty supply box in the back. Got to admit, the tiny ones were cute, though the mother looked like a huge gray rat, with some seriously sharp-looking teeth."

Annabelle couldn't help an involuntary shudder. She'd never seen an opossum in real life, but she'd seen more rats than she cared to remember. Lying awake at night, wondering if one would jump onto her bed and run across her, was one of her least favorite childhood memories.

"Um, not to be a wimp, but I don't think I'd be good at rounding up wildlife. I'd prefer scrubbing the floors on my hands and knees any day."

"Doesn't look like either one of us will have to

work on our hands and knees tonight, which is a very good thing."

She saw his gaze slide down her body and stop at her derriere, and his expression had a teasing quality to it, a little glint even, that took her by surprise and inexplicably made her heart start beating a little faster.

Stupid heart.

"Dr. Ferrera?" A small, dark-haired woman appeared in the doorway from the back room, and Daniel stepped toward her.

"Hi, Luciana. Nice to see you—it's been a long time. Thanks for seeing the child and getting this place ready. Is our patient in the back?"

"Yes, and his parents, too. How about you speak with them, then I'll send them home during the surgery?"

"Do they live close?"

"In town, so not too far. Since the surgery will take many hours, I told them they'd be more comfortable there. They didn't want to agree at first, which I understand. Perhaps you can reassure them that it's better if they go home and get some rest? That we'll contact them when it's over?"

He nodded before turning to Annabelle to introduce the two of them. From that moment on he was all business, moving into the back room to talk with the parents, who looked like they couldn't be older than twenty or so. Clearly worried, they also looked intimidated, standing to talk to Daniel when he approached them. Annabelle couldn't understand very much of what he said to them, but whatever it was had their faces relaxing slightly, their unsure expressions turning to gratitude as they both shook his hand.

Annabelle worked to get the equipment out and set up while Daniel looked at the EKG that Luciana had done, then examined the fussy baby. For long minutes he carefully listened to the child's heart and lungs with his stethoscope, his brows lowered in deep concentration.

"Definitely heart failure," he said, his gaze meeting hers. "Good thing we came. Thanks for being willing."

"No thanks necessary. You know that."

But it warmed her heart a little to be thanked anyway, silly as that was. Didn't people thank one another all the time, barely noticing it? Lord, had the man made her become all needy for a little praise? Surely she wasn't that pathetic.

Daniel listened to the infant's chest again, and even from several feet away she could hear the wheeze as he cried. Maybe the baby would have lived quite a while with congestive heart failure, but it was more likely that he wouldn't have. And that's why they did these missions, wasn't it? To save lives.

Finally, Daniel pulled his stethoscope from his ears and raised his head to look at Annabelle again. "I don't think there's any doubt it's anomalous left coronary artery from the pulmonary artery. Good call, Luciana. In an ideal world we'd do more testing, but we have no choice but to open him up and see what we find, then get it fixed."

"Ready with the gases and IVs, Doctor," Annabelle said.

He gave her a nod then shocked her with another knee-weakening smile—had he ever smiled even once in the OR at the other clinic at any of the team? She was pretty sure she would have remembered if he had. Then again, for some reason his lips and jawline and those warm brown eyes were attracting her attention in a whole new way. Something she absolutely had to squelch.

Annabelle sucked in a meditative breath as he turned away to speak to the parents again, his voice a calming rumble. More hand shaking, then the couple were gone, leaving the three of them to scrub, gown and finish prepping the space.

"Do you know this family, Luciana?"

"I didn't know them, but I do know the baby's grandmother. She goes to my church, and I'd posted there about the clinic opening in a few days, which is why they came up."

"Sounds like it was all meant to be that we're here doing this tonight. You two ready?"

Luciana nodded, and Annabelle placed the mask over the baby's nose and mouth. Once he was asleep, she put the IV lines into his tiny arms and legs, and the central line into his neck.

After carefully checking his vitals, she nodded at Daniel. "All set."

Together, they all did their jobs meticulously, with Daniel exposing the baby's small heart and beginning the intricate surgery with steady hands, Luciana assisting. "Looks like he already has some tissue death from lack of oxygen, poor little guy. But we'll get him fixed up, as close to perfect as we possibly can."

Long past midnight and hours into the surgery, Annabelle quelled a big yawn, wishing she had a giant cup of coffee. She blinked hard, briefly moving her attention from the baby's vital signs to look at Daniel's intense eyes above his surgical mask. No sign of fatigue there, just an impressive, unwavering focus.

She'd participated in many delicate and skilled surgeries, though most had been more like what they'd been doing in Ayllu, and not quite as complicated as this. And every single time she felt awed by the steady hands, the years of training it took to perform such detailed work.

She loved her job but honestly couldn't imagine doing what the cardiac surgeons did day in and day out. A special breed of doctor, for sure.

He literally held this baby's life in his hands. She did too, but it was different. Administering then carefully monitoring the anesthesia throughout surgery kept the child safe and made the procedure possible. But to be able to restructure a tiny heart so it could function normally?

Truly amazing.

He'd talked about a surgical team needing to respect one another and the admiration she felt for him at that moment welled up in her chest as she watched him work. As it did, a revelation struck her right between the eyes.

For the first time she fully understood Daniel's perspective from five years ago.

She'd made a huge mistake, there was no doubt about that. And if he, or any other surgeon, didn't feel confident that someone on their team was capable enough, the life they were responsible for could be lost. What had happened back then might have technically been partly her resident's fault, as well as her own. But when it came right down to it, the buck had stopped with her, the same way it did for a talented surgeon like Daniel.

He'd said that sometimes patients didn't get second chances. That horrible day, theirs nearly hadn't. And maybe that really did mean he'd been right. That she hadn't deserved a second chance either.

Still absorbing all that and letting it sink into her brain, she pulled her attention from the fierce focus on his face. When she looked at the baby's vital signs again, she sat straighter and stared.

"Doctor, your blood loss is ahead of where it needs to be."

"Okay. Working on it." He nodded, keeping his intent attention on his work.

Her throat tightened as she glanced at the blood-pressure monitor again, not liking one bit the continued drop in pressure. Not only did they clearly need more blood to compensate, they might need even more than she'd originally thought. Thank God she'd brought a good supply.

She hurried to retrieve a bag from the blood box, along with a second bag so it would be ready to hang if the first one didn't do the trick. Trying to work as fast as possible without making a hasty mistake, she got the first bag attached and released more blood and medicine into the child's IV lines.

"I'm having some trouble controlling the bleeding," Daniel said. "Hang another five hundred cc of blood."

"Just did. I have another one here ready to go. I'm pushing some meds to help."

For a split second his brown gaze lifted to hers, before he gave her a short, nodding salute.

"I'm going to need it. Wait just a couple minutes then go ahead and hang the second bag."

"Will do."

Relieved that the baby's blood pressure had normalized but still keeping a careful watch, the surgery took one hundred percent of Annabelle's focus. Two more hours passed until finally Daniel had the wound closed and secured, with Luciana helping to finish the bandaging. When they were ready, Annabelle removed the IV lines and slowly awakened the infant.

Daniel snapped off his gloves and pulled down his mask. The slow, deliberate way he lifted off his scrub cap showed he felt as dead tired as Annabelle did, which was hardly a surprise since it was almost 4:00 a.m. Despite the lines and shadows etched around his eyes, their brown depths looked elated as his gaze met hers for a long moment before turning to the nurse. "We did it, ladies. Luciana, great job assisting. Where have you worked?"

"I've been a surgical assistant at two different hospitals in Lima for a long time. But Huancayo is my hometown, so I was happy to come here to help get the clinic open again."

"Is there another nurse who can come here tomorrow to help care for him post-op?"

"I don't know. I'll see if I can find someone, but I'll take care of him if I can't."

"I'll also talk to Eduardo to see if he has anybody. There's no way you can take care of this little guy and deal with more patients all by yourself once the clinic is open. Not to mention you're going to need some sleep."

"All of us do," Luciana said with a tired grin. "But for tonight I'll stay here with him."

"No, we'll stay. Or I will, at least," Daniel said. "Do you have a place close by you can sleep?"

"I have relatives here, and have been staying with my mama since I arrived. I want to thank you both again for coming so fast. For being here at all. The little one might not have lived long if you hadn't decided to open the clinic. It's been closed for such a long time. I can tell you the people here appreciate it more than you can imagine."

Daniel's eyes met Annabelle's for a long moment, and she saw they were lit with emotions. Satisfaction. Appreciation. And a slight smugness that told her that he was remembering what he'd said to her when she'd been so angry about being sent off to this place to work. That when her time here was finished, she'd be glad to have taken care of the patients in need, and whether she did it at the other clinic or here didn't matter.

And, yeah, she couldn't deny she was glad.

"I need to call the parents. Do you have their number?"

Luciana recited it, and Daniel went into the other room to speak to them. Annabelle could hear his low, lilting Spanish and let herself enjoy the cadence of it, the warmth she hadn't noticed enough before.

She and Luciana again checked the baby's IV lines, oxygen, breathing and other vital signs, before finally stepping back and smiling at one another.

"Not out of the woods yet, but he seems to be doing really well," Annabelle said. "He'll have to be carefully monitored, of course, and I feel like we should stay part of the day tomorrow to help you."

"I know you have surgeries scheduled at the other clinic, but a little time here would be good. But didn't Dr. Ferrera say you were going to be here to work with Dr. Diaz at some point anyway?"

"I assume that's still the plan, but we'll see."

Maybe a certain arrogant and extremely talented surgeon was finally ready to acknowledge that she knew what she was doing, even during the most intricate surgeries.

On the other hand, maybe she should ask to come here after all. The peculiar feelings rolling around in her tummy whenever she looked at Daniel might mean working with Dr. Diaz would be a good idea.

"I told the parents there was no need for them to come back right now, that sometime in the morning would be fine as he'll be sedated for quite a while," Daniel said as he came back into the room. It seemed he was talking to both of them, but his eyes were on Annabelle.

"Isn't it already morning?" Annabelle joked, trying to cover up the way her heart pitter-pattered at the way he was looking at her. Or how she imagined he might be looking at her. In a way she shouldn't want him to be looking at her.

Or maybe she could, but for very good reasons she absolutely wasn't going to go there if he was.

One side of Daniel's mouth tipped up as he glanced at his watch. "Definitely morning. Just a couple of hours earlier than your usual wake-up time, Dr. Richards. Maybe not too early for some yoga to get you mentally centered for the day?"

"Only if you join me. I'll teach you some moves that'll help you with that grouchy controlling streak of yours."

"Moves?"

"Yoga moves," she hastily supplied, her face heating at the way the other side of his lips curved at the same time one eyebrow rose. Who would ever have thought the grim and ultraserious Dr Ferrara would make a quip like that? "A few of my favorite asana poses, then we'll end with the corpse pose to relax you."

"Corpse pose? What doctor dealing with life and death would want to do that?" He stepped closer. "Isn't there any yoga that would energize me? Because that's what I need right now."

Annabelle's stomach quivered at the teasing glint in his eyes. What in the world was happening here? Had she fallen into some alternate universe where Daniel was like a normal man and not the intense perfectionist who was always so serious?

Luciana looked from one of them to the other, obvious confusion on her face. "You wish to do yoga? I have some extra blankets in the back if you want to put them on the floor."

"No, no, Dr. Ferrera and I are just kidding. Probably. We're both half-delirious from lack of sleep."

"Yes, we all need a little sleep," Luciana said, smiling again. "There is just the one bed here, with clean sheets I put on today. Dr. Richards, you are welcome to come home with me. My mother's house is small, but we will be honored to have you take the bedroom."

Thinking about the last few minutes of strangeness, Annabelle had barely listened to what Luciana had said. Until the words *one bed* finally seeped into her brain, making it stumble in panic. No way was she sleeping in a bed with Daniel!

But she wasn't going to take Luciana's only bedroom either, and trying to get checked into a hotel room in Huancayo at 4:00 a.m. didn't seem too appealing or practical as a third option.

"Thank you so much for the kind offer but Dr. Ferrera and I will figure out the sleeping arrangement here. Don't worry about us." Though suddenly she was worrying plenty. "I guess we'll see you sometime tomorrow?"

"I just need a few hours' sleep to feel alert enough to care for the bambino. When did you say Dr. Diaz is coming here?"

"I need to double-check to see how long he thinks the travel will take," Daniel said, his expression now impassive. "I'll let you know tomorrow."

"*Adios*, then. See you about nine o'clock."

"Give yourself until ten. Still not enough sleep, but we have a pretty big patient load back at Ayllu, and we're already behind so we'll all have to work a little tired."

"Of course. Thank you again. *Buenas noches.*"

With Luciana gone, the room seemed to shrink to the size of a broom closet, the sound of the baby's oxygen machine loud and rhythmic. Daniel's eyes met hers with a magnetic pull so intense she nearly swayed forward.

"We need to get a little sleep while the baby's sedated," he said, stuffing his hands in his scrubs pockets. "The monitor will wake us up if something changes in his vital signs."

"The monitor you yelled at me about." She wanted to get back to their usual status quo. Sparks flying from arguing instead of sparks caused by something else entirely.

"I never yell. I simply pointed out that we've done more surgeries than I can count without one here." His lips curved in a slow smile that was so *not* status quo. Darn it. "But since you refuse to let the subject drop, I'll admit it. I'm glad we have it here, and it's been useful at the other clinic, too. You were smart to bring it."

She dramatically slapped her hand to her forehead, partly to hide the surprised little glow his words put in her chest. "I feel a little faint. Did you say I did something right, and that you were wrong?"

"Saying it's good we have it doesn't mean I was wrong."

"Of course not. Because you're never wrong."

His smile widened at the sound of disgust that came from her lips with her retort. "Rarely wrong. But there is one thing I was wrong about. You are an excellent anesthesiologist, and more than capable of taking care of the sickest patients during the longest surgeries. I'm impressed you caught the blood loss problem tonight, and instantly took care of it before I had to say something. So I apologize that I told you that I didn't believe you were competent enough to be a heart surgeon's anesthesiologist."

All humor and discomfort and the sarcasm she'd been giving him disappeared. Her mouth dropped open slightly and she held up her hand, catching her breath before she could finally speak. "Wait a minute. So you're saying that if you had it to do over again, you wouldn't have kept me from getting the position I wanted in Philadelphia?"

"I did what I thought was right with the information I had at the time, which was that you'd made a critical error in the middle of a serious surgery. Something you can't deny. So how did that happen?"

She looked down, not wanting to remember. Not wanting him to know any more of the details than he already did. After a long moment she forced herself to look into his eyes, steeling herself for what she'd see there. "You know it was my first month as an attending physician, wanting more than anything to get a permanent position at such an amazing hospital. It does so much good for every class of people, rich or poor, you know? It was my dream to work there. I… I wanted so much to prove myself. To impress everyone."

She paused, swallowing down the pain of that terrible day. The deep disappointment in herself that she still felt all this time later. The horrifying proof that all the people who'd told her she'd never be good enough to become a doctor had been right.

He must have seen something of what she was

feeling as he reached out to soothingly rub one hand up and down her arm as he spoke quietly. "Go on."

"You might remember that they'd placed an anesthesia resident with me that day, and I felt I needed to give him an opportunity to actually make decisions instead of just watch or follow directions, the same way one or two attendings had done for me."

"I barely remember the resident. Probably because I was concentrating on the surgery. But it's also possible that I'd only noticed the beautiful new anesthesiologist who I knew had silky blond hair tucked under her cap, captivating blue eyes, and a body any man could easily get sidetracked by."

"You noticed me?" she whispered, finding that incomprehensible. The thought made her heart beat hard in her chest. The anger she'd carried at him for all these years had pushed down the attraction she'd felt, too. Had tried to make her forget how often she'd caught herself staring at the tall, dark, cardiac surgeon with the muscular build tugging at his scrubs. Intrigued by the contrast between the all-business and often sharp man performing such detailed surgeries and the gentle doctor who'd appeared before and after when he'd spoken to his small patients and their families.

"Noticed you. Was attracted to you. Wanted to know more about you." He closed the gap between them and took both her shoulders in his hands. "So you wanted to give the resident a chance to make some decisions. But I know it was you who administered the epinephrine."

Briefly, she closed her eyes, hating to remember the biggest mistake of her career. A mistake that had nearly resulted in their patient dying. "Yes, it was me. I administered it. The resident gave me the wrong information and drew the wrong dose before handing it to me. I should have been paying closer attention, but stupidly I didn't double-check. Didn't see that he had it wrong. Until the child went into cardiac arrest, and through the flurry and panic you saved his life." Her voice dropped to a whisper. "And in my anger toward myself, which I later projected toward you, I've never given you credit for that. So thank you for saving him. I can't even imagine how it would have felt if you hadn't."

"Annabelle." He squeezed her shoulders. "It was thanks to the whole team that we brought him back."

Here he was, giving everyone credit when she'd been standing right there to see it had been his command of the situation that had brought the child back. That the way he'd immediately and expertly reacted, barking out orders to everyone, as he'd literally held the child's heart in his hand and carefully massaged it to get it beating again had been the reason the child had made it. Thinking about her failure to monitor the resident and double-check the dose the way she should have made her feel sick all over again. Made her fall into the deep well of inadequacy she'd felt her whole life. That she'd fought so hard to climb out of to become the best doctor she possibly could be.

"It was my mistake," she said looking into his

eyes, her stomach knotting, knowing she'd see disdain there again. The condemnation she deserved. "My screw-up. The resident was my responsibility as much as the patient was. But I didn't want anyone to know that, after all my hard work, I still wasn't good enough. I... I did make myself admit it to the hospital administrators and senior anesthesiologist, hoping to get to stay on. To have one more chance to prove myself. I just never admitted it to you."

Unexpected and very unwelcome tears stung her eyes, and she tried to swing away, hating to show that kind of weakness. She never cried. Had learned not to cry from the time she'd been little, because it just made people around you impatient or angry, and it never accomplished one thing other than to make your throat hurt and your nose run.

"Annabelle, it's over and done with, and you need to let it go. As I'm going to." Daniel moved his hands from her shoulders to wrap them loosely around her, folding her against his broad chest. "Making mistakes during surgery is something I have little tolerance for, as you know. But we are all human, and when we do make mistakes, all we can do is learn from them."

"You don't make mistakes. Does that mean you're not human?"

"I'm very human." His voice lowered as he drew her closer and, yes, he did feel very, very human. Warm and masculine, and she leaned against his hard chest, even as she told herself she shouldn't. "I've made a few mistakes that I've made sure never to make again. And I'm willing to bet that you'll never work with a resident again without watching everything they do like they were a bug under a microscope."

That had her sniffing and giving a slight, watery chuckle. "I've been told residents moan about working with me. Didn't realize I was making them feel like bugs. And here I always thought it was you with the reputation for being stern and verbally slapping people in the OR."

"Maybe we're more alike than either of us would have ever thought, hmm?"

"Maybe we are." She lifted her head to stare

up at him. "And I confess I'm not sure if that's horrifying or flattering."

"I'm not sure either." A slight smile softened his lips and then, to her shock, he lowered them to hers, a light, soft touch that moved so slowly it left her straining close for more, and sent her heart into long, heavy thuds against her ribs.

The arms that had held her loosely tightened, pressing her breasts to his chest and her hips to his as his mouth deepened its exploration of hers, stroking and coaxing until she gasped with the pleasure of it. The dizzying taste of him, the stroke of his tongue in her mouth and the heat coming from his body had her wrapping her arms around his neck and hanging on. Sent her fingers into his short, soft hair to caress him and hold his mouth in place. His hands moved on her, slowly sliding to her waist and up her ribs, down to the base of her spine and up to cup her breast, the sensation so incredible she found herself shaking with the goodness of it.

The shriek of the monitor sent them practically jumping apart, and for one long moment they just stared at one another, breathing hard, until they wordlessly moved to turn off the alarm and check on the infant.

She dropped her hand from the monitor, shaking as she watched Daniel touch the baby and study his vital signs, to figure out what had triggered the alarm.

What had she been thinking? She couldn't kiss Daniel, let her attraction to him dull her common sense. Not only had animosity been the cornerstone of their relationship up to now, he was from rich, upper-crust Peruvian society and she was from dirt. The last thing she'd ever want would be to fall for another guy whose family would be horrified to find out who she really was.

Been there, done that. There'd been a time when part of her had hoped, dreamed that her accomplishments were enough. That today was what mattered, that she could keep her past hidden and buried. A different part of her sometimes wanted to shout to the world about how hard she'd scrabbled, becoming a doctor despite the odds stacked very much against her.

But in college and beyond she'd learned it often didn't work that way. That if people found out, they either felt sorry for her or judged her. Or pretended to admire her then avoided her. Found her lacking or pathetic somehow, the way they had her entire life.

Throughout her childhood it had hurt when practically every person she'd known had looked down on her, doubted her, kept clear of her. It still hurt today.

No, it was best to keep to herself, to spend her time making a difference in the lives of disadvantaged kids like she had been. And if she ever did find someone she wanted to be involved with? He needed to be from a similar, sad background. A man who wouldn't be shocked to learn she wasn't who he'd thought she was.

Super surgeon Daniel Ferrera was not that man.

CHAPTER FIVE

"LOOKS LIKE HIS oxygen saturation is a little low," Daniel said, knowing he sounded breathless but unable to help it after that searing kiss. After the way it had obliterated thoughts of anything but the intense sexual desire that had surged through every part of his body as their mouths had devoured one another. Desire that had been just seconds away from dancing her over to that small bed, stripping her naked and making love with her all night, and to hell with getting any sleep.

"Could be laryngospasm."

He nearly smiled at the shakiness of her voice and the deep breath she'd taken before she'd tried to talk. Obviously, he wasn't the only one feeling the heat. "Could be. But first I'll check for airway obstruction while you get a mask on him again."

"All right. If it looks like laryngospasm, I'd like

to try a light plane of anesthesia before we consider extubating."

The woman was one smart doctor, and as their eyes met briefly he hoped she saw he knew that now. "Agreed."

He carefully moved the tube in the child's throat, peering at it. "Nothing visible as far as obstruction is concerned. Hopefully it'll improve, giving him oxygen. If not, we'll go with the anesthesia first."

"I see this a lot in infants post-op, as I'm sure you know," Annabelle said, her pretty face in profile as she held the mask to the baby's face then glanced at the monitor. "But look. It's already slightly improved. We'll give it some time before we decide on the next step."

"Agreed."

Their eyes met over the baby's small face, and Daniel's lips twisted in a wry smile. "I'm not sure I think the monitor was a good idea anymore. That sound interrupted the best kiss I've had in a long time." Maybe even the best kiss he'd ever had in his entire life, though he wasn't going to admit that.

"And here I was thinking it proved even more that it was a good thing I brought it."

"You weren't enjoying our kiss?"

"You know I was," she said, her eyes meeting his again, and their color reminded him of a deep lake high in the Andes that he and his brother had swum in as children. "But we now managed to achieve a more cordial working relationship and you've scheduled us to work at different clinics, and I have that crucial meeting to arrange."

"Not sure I'm clear on what all that has to do with me kissing you. With wanting another." And he did want another kiss, or ten. Seeing where that might lead sounded better than good.

Her lips twisted. "I know you probably have quickie things with women all the time but I'm just not that kind of woman. Plus, if we work together in Ayllu even just one more day, we might get…involved again while we're there. Maybe make the rest of the team uncomfortable. It just isn't a good idea, and you know it."

"You're sure a quickie thing tonight and tomorrow doesn't sound like a pretty damn good thing? Because it does to me."

That was met with a deep frown, reminding him of the Annabelle he was used to. He had to smile even as he was disappointed, knowing she was going to shoot down his suggestion.

"Not a good thing. Not to mention that it's going on four thirty in the morning and we have patients to see in no time. You really want to do surgeries after just a few hours of sleep?"

"I have before." He folded his arms across his chest and sighed, since it was clear she wasn't going to be charmed into a few hours of great sex. "What meeting is this you have to get to?"

She glanced down at the baby. "I have a business thing I need to talk to some people about. If I leave Peru without that happening, there's a very good chance it'll be too late. And it's something important I've wanted to make happen for a long time."

"When is it?"

"Well—" her pretty lips twisted in a wry smile

"—it was supposed to be the first day I got to Lima, coming to the clinic the next day. But you already know what happened there."

"Have you tried to reschedule it?"

"Several times. But the number one decision maker left the country the next day, and I'm waiting to hear back."

Daniel was curious what important business meeting could be happening between an American doctor and someone in Peru, but the way she'd sidetracked from what it was made it clear she wasn't sharing.

"Well, I hope you hear from him soon." A yawn sneaked up on him that he couldn't stop and, as often happened, Annabelle yawned, too, and they both laughed.

"See? I'm right, as usual. We need some shut-eye. You go ahead and sleep, and I'll stay up with the baby to keep an eye on him," she said.

"That monitor is quite loud enough to wake us if his vitals are off again. We should both catch a few hours' sleep so we can be conscious enough to do at least one surgery tomorrow afternoon when we get back to Ayllu. Looks like the bed has plenty of blankets for both of us."

The blue gaze that met his turned utterly serious. "I don't think it's a good idea for us to sleep together."

"Annabelle, it would just be *sleeping*. I promise. You've told me loud and clear you're not interested in anything else. And since I'm dead on my feet, and I know you are, too, we'll both probably be out in about twenty seconds flat." Actually, he wasn't sure that was true, as knowing her warm, beautiful body was mere inches from his would definitely make falling asleep hard. Along with other things. But either way they needed to try to catch a few winks, if only so they didn't run off the road on the drive back.

"I'll just sleep on the floor with a couple of the extra blankets," she said.

"And risk being eaten by an opossum?"

A look of horror so extreme it was comical landed on her face, and he almost laughed. Then had to choke it down a second time as she looked all around the floor like she might actually see one.

"There's nothing in here. Right? Luciana cleaned the place and she wouldn't leave critters in here during a surgery. Would she?"

"You never know." She looked so genuinely scared his amusement died. "Annabelle, I'm kidding. If there were any animals in here, we'd know it by now. But if anyone's going to sleep on the floor, it's going to be me."

Her teeth sank into her soft lower lip as she obviously struggled with what to do. It was glaringly obvious that the thought of sleeping on the floor gave her the creeps, but she also clearly didn't want him to either. Was the thought of them sharing that bed so horrifying?

Apparently it was.

Since he wasn't the kind of man who'd want to make love with a woman who wasn't sure she wanted to or make her feel uncomfortable by sharing a bed, he grabbed the extra blankets and a worn but clean-looking pillow and laid them on the floor. There was no point in wasting more good sleeping time talking about this, especially as it was clear he wasn't going to get lucky tonight. "Go to bed, Annabelle. I'll see you in the morning."

The day of surgeries in Ayllu was hard to get through, with Annabelle feeling a serious need for a nap. Between patients, and during surgery when things were going smoothly, she found herself looking at Daniel to see how he was holding up. Not, of course, because she was thinking any more about that kiss between them. Thinking about how, despite being exhausted, it had been hard to get to sleep last night. Thinking about how nice it would have been to lie close to his warm body, his soft breathing just feet away making her want to roll onto the floor and snuggle with him. And to heck with any opossums.

Not a good idea, she'd reminded herself a dozen times until she'd finally fallen asleep.

The brown eyes above his mask looked as fatigued as she felt, but no naps could be on the agenda with a full patient load they both were committed to getting through.

As Karina prepared to wheel the last patient to Recovery, Daniel sent the team a tired smile. "Another good day. Thanks for hanging in there." His gaze lifted to Annabelle's and his lips curved a little more. "I was afraid you might fall asleep over there, since you refused to catch some shut-eye in the car on the way back here."

"Because there was no way I could close my eyes and relax while you took hairpin turns at top speed."

"You forget I've driven these roads a lot over the years. You can trust me."

Maybe when it came to his driving. But when it came to their newfound friendship and the sexual attraction simmering between them? Better not to trust him or herself.

"Uh-huh. I can only hope that Dr. Diaz's driving is less scary than yours when he takes me back to Huancayo. Did he say when he and Dr. Velasco will be here?"

A frown formed between his eyes. "He said

there's been a delay. Probably not for another day or two."

A sharp little stab struck in the region of her heart at his expression, which said he was greatly bothered by that news. Hadn't he said last night that he'd become convinced that she was capable of delivering anesthesia to the most critical patients? Had he only said that because he'd wanted some "quickie thing" with her and not because he'd really meant it?

"Anyway, I want to talk to you some more about that plan after dinner," he said, his eyes seeming to study her.

When his frown lines deepened she quickly put on her game face, getting rid of whatever he might be seeing there. The last thing she'd ever want would be for him to think of her as some clingy, needy woman still looking for his approval. Hadn't she learned long ago that wanting approval from anyone just brought pain and disappointment most of the time?

"I'll be here." She shrugged, going for nonchalant and indifferent to whatever he had to say.

She didn't want anything from him. In fact, if he was thinking it was unfortunate that the two doctors weren't going to be here as soon as they'd originally thought, she couldn't agree more. The sooner she went to Huancayo, away from spending all day working with Daniel then sharing meals and conversation, the better.

"I'm going to go over tomorrow's schedule and talk with patients and their families over at Administration. See you at the hotel later."

Annabelle caught herself watching him move out the door, completely unable to not admire how broad his shoulders were and how great his tush looked in scrubs. To forget how it had felt when he'd held her warm and close against all that sexiness.

Stop it.

Snapping her attention back to the equipment she needed to clean and sterilize, Jennifer dumped a second batch of tubing into the sink and leaned close to her.

"Okay, what happened in Huancayo?" Jennifer's low voice and eyebrow waggling gave

Annabelle's heart a little jolt. Had she made it obvious that Daniel was off her list of most disliked people and had somehow rushed to number one on her list of hunky men she couldn't stop thinking about?

"I told you. The baby did have ALCAPA and—"

"Not what I'm talking about and you know it. All day, the simmering looks between you and our hunky cardiac doc were so intense I had to make sure I didn't step in the middle somehow for fear I might get singed."

So much for hoping no one had noticed the zing between them. She didn't even want to think about how much more zing would have sizzled in the room if they'd done anything more than just sleep.

"I don't know what you're talking about. Except we did have a conversation about what happened five years ago. I admitted my mistake, and he told me he'd come to realize that I'm pretty good at my job."

"And he's also come to realize that you are gorgeous and smart and fun. Though I think he knew the gorgeous part all along. While you've also come to realize he's smart, super good looking and his intensity is just part of his charm."

"If you say so." She hung some of the tubing on the line and sighed, knowing Jennifer wasn't going to give up until she gave her some kind of real answer. "Fine. We were alone and talking about the past and then we ended up kissing. It was a surprise and…and very pleasant. Then we agreed that would be the only time. Nothing more than that, and no big deal." Okay, *pleasant* wasn't even close to the right word to describe it, but she wasn't going to use the word *spectacular*.

"Yeah, right." Apparently she hadn't come close to convincing Jennifer either because her friend let out a loud snort. "You forget I know you pretty well. Ever think that maybe all that animosity between the two of you was really a blazing chemistry all along? I can't remember a time when I've seen you look at a guy the way you look at Dr. Ferrera."

"I don't want to be looking at him any way but as a colleague."

"Except you are," Jennifer said softly. She wrapped her arm around Annabelle's shoulders and gave her a hug. "You haven't been involved with a guy in a long time. All work and no play isn't good for anybody, spending all your time at the hospital back home, or the free clinic, or working on your school plans. Why not let yourself see what might be there between you two?"

"It would never work. He told me he's from a rich Peruvian family and you know where I come from. Two steps down from dirt."

"Just because that stupid guy you dated in college had snobby parents who disapproved of you when they found out how you'd grown up doesn't mean most people are like that."

"Maybe not, but why risk it? I'd never fit in with a family like that anyway." She'd learned long ago how true that was, and had to believe Jennifer understood that, too. "If I ever have a long-term relationship with a man, I want it to be with someone like me. Someone who doesn't really have family. Who picked themselves up from the ground and has an interest in making life better for kids like us. Someone who would support me emotionally as I get the school up and running, maybe even help to mentor the kids who've never had good role models. Someone who understands all that stuff."

"I think you're assuming things. And maybe you're not being fair to Daniel, not giving him a chance to show you who he really is, other than wealthy and a great surgeon."

"Even if I was willing to do that, a relationship isn't what he's after and I'm just not a fling kind of person. I don't even want to think about how many different men my mother spent time with in her lifetime."

"Annabelle, you are not, and never will be, anything like your mother, and you know it." Jennifer cocked her head at her, studying her until Annaabelle felt like squirming. "All right. I'll drop the subject for now. But I want you to promise me you'll think about what I said."

Since her goal was to shut down any and all thoughts about Daniel, she wasn't promising anything. "Looks like this is the last stuff to clean and sterilize. I don't suppose you'll let me eat in my room to avoid Dr. Ferrera? Maybe you and I could have a quiet night there, playing Scrabble."

"Except you always soundly beat me, and I'm tired of having my ego pummeled." Jennifer grinned. "How about Euchre, with two docs and two nurses teamed up? Maybe you'd be so busy staring into one another's eyes, Karina and I would have a chance to win."

Annabelle rolled her eyes, at the same time grimacing. Because, yeah, that would probably be exactly how it would go. "No games. Now that I think about it, my bed is calling me to an early night."

"Are you sure it isn't calling you for something else?"

"Really appreciate your support here, Jen." She scowled and shoved open the door, with Jennifer's laughter following behind her as she headed towards the hotel.

She wasn't about to admit that her friend's words put images in her brain she didn't want there, but at the same time her tingling body seemed to want to enjoy those images very much.

No, there seemed to be only one thing she was sure of. That she felt totally confused.

CHAPTER SIX

THE NEXT MORNING'S surgeries came rapidly, one after the other, without leaving time to think about anything but their patients. Daniel figured Annabelle had probably been glad about that since she'd hurried ahead of everyone when it was time to break for lunch and he doubted it was because she was extra-hungry.

She was half-done by the time he sat down with his meal, and he watched her gobble her lunch with even more gusto than usual. Yeah, there was no doubt it was more about her wanting to be done and out of the hotel dining room than her enjoyment of the meal.

His fault. He'd made her feel uncomfortable when he'd admitted he wanted to make love with her. Looking back, he probably shouldn't have taken advantage of the two of them being all alone in the middle of the night. Talking then kissing in a room that had only one fairly small bed.

But he hadn't been able to resist. When her sweet face had looked up into his, vulnerability and guilt filling her misty eyes as she'd confessed her error and how bad she felt about it, he'd lowered his mouth to hers before he'd known he was going to. And the second his lips had touched hers, he was gone. All he'd been able to think about was the taste of her and the feel of her and how much he wanted to see her naked. To touch every inch of her soft skin and make love with her until the pain and scare and disappointment in herself on that harrowing day were forgotten.

If the baby monitor hadn't gone off, he knew he would have taken it further, and had a feeling she wouldn't have resisted. But since she'd now told him loud and clear that she didn't do flings, and the only thing he could offer a woman was short-term companionship and lovemaking, anything between them was out of the question.

Except apparently a part of his mind and body

kept forgetting that, as he couldn't seem to keep his eyes off her. Couldn't seem to keep what he was thinking off his face, and since she'd quickly turn away every time their eyes met, she obviously saw it plain as day.

Since her attention was now firmly on her plate, he furtively watched her eat, thinking about her lips and how they'd tasted, something he couldn't get out of his head, no matter how hard he tried. A conversation between Jennifer and Karina vaguely touched his ears before he heard the sudden, insistent ringing of a phone. Annabelle practically jumped from her chair, pulled her phone from her pocket and hurried toward the front door.

"I need to take this."

Even as he tried to make small talk with the other women, his mind was on Annabelle and her call. Was it the person she'd been wanting to hear from so much? Was she getting her meeting set up in Lima and, if so, when would that happen? Or could it be a boyfriend she hadn't told him about? Was that the root of her reluctance to take things further?

They were still behind on the number of surgeries they'd wanted to get done, and he hoped she wouldn't need to leave for a bit. And also, damn it, because he'd realized he'd miss seeing her, and working with her, and talking with her. His stomach burned a little, and he didn't think it was from the meal. He had a feeling it was the thought that she might be dating someone, though surely, if she was, she'd have told him. A boyfriend was the best reason in the world to avoid letting another man kiss you and touch you, so that couldn't be it.

He rubbed his hand down his face. How had they gone from barely being civil to one another to him thinking about her all the time? To feeling this intense need to be with her, even if it was just to look into her intelligent eyes and see her smile?

On the drive back from Huancayo, he'd decided that he'd ask her to stay here after Eduardo and Alan showed up. Would just have the two of them go on to Huancayo, instead of Annabelle and Eduardo. He'd told her he had confidence in her because he'd meant it, and he couldn't deny they worked well together.

Except the way she'd avoided talking to him much of the day made him wonder if she'd tell him she wanted to go to Huancayo anyway.

The longer she was gone the more restless he felt, until he excused himself and went outside, hoping she wouldn't be annoyed with him for butting in. But she'd told him about trying to set up some kind of meeting and how important it was to her, right? Surely she'd appreciate his interest. If that was even what the phone call was about.

The sight of her beautiful round bottom bending over in her scrubs had him coming to an abrupt stop to stare. To fantasize again, this time picturing walking over there and putting his hands on her hips and pulling her back against him, to feel her softness against his hardness while he nuzzled her neck, kissed her earlobe, turned her around to—

Damn. He turned to stare at the trees, to suck in a deep breath and cool the heat he kept feeling when he was around her. When he finally had his thoughts and body under control, he cleared his throat. She stood, turning in surprise as a small cat wound itself around her leg. Even from a few yards away, the happy purring was audible.

"You're feeding that cat again? If you get the whole team booted out of this place, we're going to have to sleep out here on the ground and, let me tell you, I'm not keen to do that again."

A guilty smile lit her eyes as she chuckled. "I'd confess it was me. I wouldn't really tell them it was you feeding it."

"Uh-huh. With the payback you doubtless want to give me, I'm not sure I believe that."

"No paybacks. I thought we were done with all that." She clutched her hands together and stared up at him. "But I do have to talk to you about something. That was the call I've been worrying about. I'm so relieved I got this meeting set up, but I have to go to Lima to make it happen. I'm really sorry, since I messed up our schedule from the very beginning, and here I'm about to do it again. But I'm afraid you'll have to just see patients this afternoon for things other than surgery until I get back sometime tomorrow."

"When's your meeting?"

"It's this afternoon then another tomorrow morning, with a couple more people joining us." She gnawed her lip. "I'm really sorry to leave you high and dry like this, and it's totally my own fault that I missed the first meeting there. But it's really important, and I expect I'll be back fairly early tomorrow, or at least by midday."

"You're leaving soon?"

"I have to. Two thirty is the only time they could squeeze me in. I'm going to call a cab then take a quick shower. I hope they don't take a long time to get here or I might be doomed again."

A vision of her all wet and sudsy flashed in his brain before he forcibly shut it off. "Then what? Stay in a hotel after your meeting?"

"Well, there must be plenty of hotels there, right?" Her white teeth sank into her lush lip. "I've never spent time in Lima, just drove through from the airport. I don't suppose you have a suggestion for a place for me to stay?"

"You've never been there?"

"Not really. Never did any touristy stuff, since I've always spent the time I have at the mission clinics outside the city. Maybe Karina would know about hotels there I could call that would be close to the hospital. I'll go ask her."

"So you don't have a place to stay and you're hightailing it to Lima to make this mystery meeting happen." Right then and there, he decided he was going be involved in this excursion whether she liked it or not. Being all alone in a place where she had no clue where she was going was not a good idea. "How about you tell me about this meeting."

"It's for a project of mine."

"Why do I feel like you've been strangely secretive about this from the beginning?" He folded his arms across his chest, deciding to play hard ball with her. "You're leaving your job here to make this meeting happen, and we all have to adjust what we do here while you're gone. I think I have a right to know why you have to go."

Her blue eyes clung to his in obvious indecision. Her chest lifted as she drew breath and held it, and he tried hard not to get sidetracked by her beautiful body beneath those loose scrubs. Finally, she exhaled in a sound of defeat. "Fine. There's an inner-city school in Chicago that serves underprivileged kids that's being closed. Going to be torn down in a couple months. I want to buy it and turn it into a charter school that specializes in introducing high school kids to various health services fields, from techs to phlebotomy, nursing, pharmacy, all kinds of things. Show kids who have no role models that they can do good things and have a good career in medicine. Even become a doctor if they work hard enough."

"What does this have to do with Lima? Peru?"

"These kids in Chicago think they've got the worst lives in the world. I want them to travel, to see that some people have equally difficult challenges in some other countries, like the people we treat here." She waved her arm toward the clinic and OR. "I have a number of donors lined up in Chicago, but I need more. A hospital there said they'd help finance it and get involved in the exchange program I pitched to them if I found a partner here. US kids going to the charter school would spend time in Lima to learn and work at the hospital, and Peruvian kids would spend time at the school and hospital in Chicago. It would open up a whole new world to all of them. Teach them to believe in a future and in themselves that most never believe in at all."

Her expression was equal parts fierce determination, anxious worry and something else. He couldn't tell what it was, but it almost seemed like...shame?

No, that couldn't be right. Her ideas, her goals impressed him more than anything had in a long time.

"That's quite a concept. One I can get on board with. And since I want to know more about it, and don't want you to miss your meeting, I'll take you."

"What?" She stared at him in obvious shock.

"No, I'm fine to take a cab. Really. I don't want to take you away from patients. Please don't worry about it."

"I can't do surgeries without an anesthesiologist. Karina and Jennifer can see patients in the clinic and have more time caring for our post-op patients until we get back."

"I...don't know what to say."

"That it's a good idea? Not having to wait for a taxi will ensure you get to the meeting in plenty of time and also ensures you'll get back in a timely manner tomorrow for the surgeries we have lined up."

"Well, if you put it that way, I guess it is a good idea." Her expression didn't match her words, as it was clear she wasn't very sure about any of it. "Thank you. Do you know of a hotel where we can stay? In separate rooms," she added hastily.

"Don't worry, Annabelle. You've told me loud and clear how you feel about sharing a room or a bed." Part of him wanted to laugh but at the same time he wished it could be different. "My grandparents have an apartment in Miraflores, where they live when they're not at their other home in Paracas."

"So you'd stay there?"

"I need to visit my grandparents anyway. Usually, I see them for a day or two after a mission trip like this, but if I go now, it'll kill two birds with one stone, as the saying goes. I'll drop you off at the hospital for your meeting, then we'll stay the night with my grandparents. I'll visit with them a little longer while you have your second meeting in the morning, then we'll drive back."

"We?" Her voice rose to a squeak. "Stay with your grandparents? Both of us?"

She looked stunned and alarmed, and he supposed he couldn't blame her. Had it been just days ago that they'd held each other in great dislike?

But, of course, he'd never disliked her. The problem between them had only been about their patients and Daniel's past that had molded him into the man he was.

"Neither one of us will have to sleep on the

floor, I promise. Believe me, I'd go to a hotel instead, if that were the case." He sent her a smile, hoping she'd see it would be fine. "Their apartment has plenty of room. They'll be happy to see me and interested to meet you."

"Well..." She frowned, her eyes full of indecision. "I admit it sounds nice to not have to figure out where to stay. But I really don't want to inconvenience you. Or your grandparents."

"No inconvenience for me or them, I promise. I believe in this project and would like to learn more about it."

"Well, all right. Thank you. I'm just...so glad that this meeting is actually going to happen, and I appreciate your help." The doubt was still clear on her face, warring with a relieved smile. "When do you want to leave?"

"As soon as we get cleaned up and packed. It's not a long way to Lima from here, but part of the road isn't the best, as you know, and traffic is unpredictable close to the city."

"I'll be back in the lobby in twenty minutes."

He watched her hurry into the hotel and wondered why his chest felt strangely light, even happy, as though the two of them were going on some minivacation together, when in truth they couldn't exactly linger in Miraflores so he could show her his favorite places there, take her to a few of the great restaurants. The thought of that made him smile, imagining her expression, how her beautiful mouth would look while she savored delicious, five-star food instead of the modest hotel fare they'd been dining on. To relax and spend time on the beach with her, finally getting to see more of the lush body that he couldn't stop fantasizing about.

He mentally smacked himself. What was he talking about? She didn't want a fling with him, and he'd never spent vacation time with a woman as platonic friends, though the images in his mind appealed so much that maybe Annabelle would be the exception.

Again, he shook his head, wondering what was wrong with him. Work called, with the line of children needing surgery getting longer every day as they fell further behind with their schedule.

Fun and relaxation could not be on the agenda, even if Annabelle was willing to enjoy that kind of time with him.

Which she wouldn't be, anyway. The woman was not interested in him. The image he'd just painted in his mind of being with her outside the hospital, of simply relaxing and enjoying one another's company was never going to happen. Even as he couldn't get the taste of her mouth out of his head, she'd made it clear she never wanted to think about their kiss again.

Annabelle tried to sit still as she waited in the hospital's cavernous meeting room, but couldn't seem to control the jiggling of her knee and the twitching nerves. Finally, she just couldn't sit there any longer and got up to pace in front of the wide window overlooking the tall, modern skyline of downtown Lima.

All the words she'd tried to rehearse for her presentation seemed to be only half there, and she had a feeling it wasn't just because of the importance of this meeting and how much she wanted to make her lofty goal happen.

No, the truth was that a lot of it had to do with Daniel. Keeping her focus on him strictly professional had become hard enough when they were in the OR, or caring for patients, or, even worse, when they were sitting together at meals, despite Karina and Jennifer being there with them.

Sharing the intimacy of a car ride cocooning them together was a whole other story. That had been nerve-racking enough when they'd driven to Huancayo. But now that they'd shared that searing kiss, sitting so close made her hyperaware of him. Of his size, his chiseled profile, his delicious scent.

She paced the room again. Somehow she had to find some mental distance for the times they didn't have a physical distance between them. Like tomorrow, when the ride back would doubtless be as torturous as today's journey had been.

If only Dr. Diaz and Dr. Velasco would finally show up at the clinic. Just days ago she'd been furious with Daniel setting that up. Angry and hurt.

Now she couldn't wait to work at the other clinic. Memories of Daniel and that kiss and how all that had felt would fade into the distance. Probably she'd never work with him again, and even as she tried to feel relieved by that, a part of her felt a little sad.

She pressed her fingers to her eyes. Why in the world would she feel even a pinch sad? Daniel had told her he wasn't looking for a forever-after kind of relationship, but even if he was, she wasn't the right woman for him. Where you came from mattered, and that was that.

Annoyed with herself, she stretched her arms toward the ceiling and drew deep breaths in an effort to get rid of this unwelcome anxiety. After a few minutes she felt more normal, deciding to go over the papers she'd brought so she'd be ready to launch into her pitch when the two men arrived.

If they ever did. She glanced at her watch, starting to get a little worried that there might be a reason the mayor of Lima and the director of this hospital weren't here yet. Surely they hadn't forgotten about the appointment, since they'd scheduled it with her only hours ago.

The door swung open, and she sagged in relief as two men walked into the room. She moved toward them, reaching out her hand with a smile she hoped looked relaxed. That didn't show how her stomach felt all bunched up with nerves.

"Hello. Dr. Loyola? Mr. Oros? I'm Dr. Annabelle Richards. I so appreciate you meeting with me today, especially since I know it was an effort to reschedule it. I'm so sorry I ended up missing our first meeting."

"Not a problem, Dr. Richards," Mr. Oros said. "We're just glad we managed to connect while you're here. We certainly know all about missed connections and difficult travel."

"Yes, we do," the hospital director agreed with a grin. "We are happy you reached out to us. The idea of a collaboration between the disadvantaged youth of Chicago and those here in Peru is intriguing to both Mr. Oros and me. Certainly offering them opportunities to consider some aspect of medicine and health care as a career is an excellent idea. The secretary of education here is also very interested to talk with you, and he's looking forward to joining us in the morning."

"That is so good to hear." Her chest felt buoyant now, as cautious optimism shoved away her nerves. "I've outlined the curriculum that groups of kids from our area and here would have at the schools, taking health-related classes in addition to regular classwork."

She handed them the extensive urban studies curriculum from both Lima and the United States, and the plan she'd worked on for over a year, as they sat at the table together. "This joint program would give kids education, vision and opportunity, with mentorship from medical professionals and participation in the exchange program between the two cities."

Annabelle wiped her hands on her skirt several times as the men perused the documents and asked her questions. She hadn't even realized until this moment how much she truly wanted this to happen. Knew, deep in her gut, that it would be an amazing program that would literally change the lives of young people both here and in Chicago. That if it was successful, it could even be expanded into other cities and other countries, with a ripple effect that could well be immeasurable.

Her own life had been changed by one single person, and now it was her turn to change others' lives.

A hard knock on the closed door had all three of them looking up when it abruptly opened. The woman who'd shown her to this room before stood there, and Annabelle's mouth fell open with surprise when she saw Daniel standing behind her.

The woman began speaking in Spanish, but Daniel strode into the room, interrupting her.

"My apologies for intruding, but Dr. Richards and I have an emergency at the Ayllu clinic we must get to immediately. We might be too late, but have to try."

"What is it?" Carlos Loyola stood and gave Daniel's hand a quick shake.

"One of the nurses at the clinic contacted me

to say we have a man with an abdominal aortic aneurism. He arrived with severe back and belly pain. After feeling pulsating near his navel, she did an ultrasound. Confirmed a large aneurism, eight centimeters."

"Damn." Dr. Loyola pulled his phone from his pocket. "We'll have the hospital helicopter take you. No way you'll get there in time if you have to drive."

Daniel gave a short nod. "Thank you. If he lives he'll need to be in the ICU. Could you have the chopper come back for him after surgery?"

"Will do." After a quick conversation, he looked up. "The chopper's getting ready for you now. Dr. Richards, we'll still see you in the morning? Maybe extend our meeting so we can go over the materials a little more since we can't do that right now."

"That would be good. If that's okay?" She looked at Daniel, wondering if he'd feel frustrated by her taking yet another trek away from the clinic after they were having to rush back.

"It won't delay the surgery schedule much more than we'd already planned for."

"Of course, that's fine." He gave her a quick nod, his gaze intense. "Let's go. There might not be a second to lose."

"I'm ready."

They rushed out the door, and the stab of distress she felt that she hadn't been able to conclude the meeting with some kind of answer lasted only a split second because Daniel was right. With so few people surviving that size abdominal aortic aneurism before surgery, and even fewer post-op, how fast they got there might literally mean the difference between life and death.

CHAPTER SEVEN

DANIEL WATCHED ANNABELLE as she stared out the window of the chopper, barely noting the rugged landscape that he rarely got to see from this view. His thoughts were focused on two things— the survival of their patient and her.

When he'd first seen her walk into the hotel lobby earlier, his heart had kicked in his chest at the navy-blue dress she wore. It emphasized her curves despite it being businesslike and demure, and made her hair seem an even lighter blond, like corn silk in the sunlight. The outfit proved that, sexy as the woman looked in scrubs, she looked even better in clothes that showed off her gorgeous legs. Then he'd had to suffer looking at those legs and wanting to reach over to touch her soft skin the entire car ride to Lima. He wanted to keep looking at them even now.

"I've never flown in a helicopter before," Annabelle said, shoving her hair behind her ears in a nervous gesture. "It's kind of scary, don't you think?"

"Are you feeling scared?" He let himself reach for her hand, wishing he'd noticed instead of being so focused on her body and his own feelings of lust he needed to control. "Just look at me, then, and not out the window. We'll be there soon."

"I know it's silly. I mean, flying's flying, right? It doesn't bother me to travel in a plane, you know?"

"We're sitting in a loud, glass bubble where you can see in three directions. It's getting darker, and I don't know about you but the mix of sun and cloud shadows on the trees and mountains and rivers looks a little eerie, don't you think? Makes one ponder what it would be like to crash-land into all that wilderness."

He said it in a teasing voice, and the hand he wasn't holding smacked his arm.

"What a way to reassure a girl. Thanks ever so much."

"You're welcome." He leaned over to look out her side of the chopper, breathing in her scent and wishing he could kiss her fears away. "If you try to think about how beautiful it is, though, how awesome the landscape is and how you might not ever see it this way again, it'll help you feel calm and even enjoy it some."

"I'll try."

"Or do some of your yoga that helps you get mentally centered."

"Yoga in a helicopter? Might be a little problematic."

That his joke brought a smile to her face warmed his chest and made him smile, too. Her gaze met his for a long moment as she squeezed his hand, and it surprised and pleased him that she didn't pull away. Probably because she needed the reassurance of someone's touch, nothing more.

After a few more minutes the pilot told them they were heading down and brought the helicopter to a near stop in the sky before slowly descending to a fairly flat open space not too far from the clinic.

"Unbelievable that he can do that!" Annabelle said, her eyes becoming round. "Just hover in midair."

"They go in reverse, too. I'd ask him to show you, except we're kind of in a hurry."

Her smile faded as she nodded. He grabbed both their bags in one hand and jumped from the helicopter, turning to reach for her. The rotors sent her silky hair flying across her face, and he couldn't help but wrap his arm around her shoulders as they ducked and ran toward the clinic.

As he'd expected, Jennifer and Karina had the patient completely ready to go in the OR, with all the surgical equipment and items for the anesthesia carefully laid out on the stainless-steel side table. He and Annabelle threw on surgical gowns and scrubbed as fast as possible while getting the information they needed.

"How are his vitals, and what's his hemoglobin?"

"Not good. Barely conscious. BP is sixty over

basically nothing," Jennifer said. "Pulse is one-forty, hemoglobin six."

"All right, let's get him some blood and to sleep, fast," Annabelle said, grabbing the IV, anesthesia mask and gases.

"Just tell me when," Daniel said as he prepped the abdomen for the incision.

"Almost there. Hold on." He watched her get the IV in place with remarkable speed and precision, before she looked up at him. "Okay. So what are you waiting for?"

"Obviously not for you, Doctor." His lips quirked as he started the incision just below the sternum all the way down to the pubic symphysis. Once he entered the peritoneal cavity, the immediate rush of blood was stunning. He had to get the flow stopped fast or the patient might bleed out, and he concentrated on getting the aorta clamped above the leak. He glanced at the monitor, relieved to see the pressure quickly stabilize as the blood stopped draining through the rupture in the wall of the large vessel.

"Wow," Annabelle said breathlessly as she continued to systematically pump blood into the patient to compensate for all he'd lost. "I don't think I've ever seen that much blood volume flowing where it shouldn't be. Incredible how fast you got it clamped, Dr. Ferrera. You absolutely saved his life just now."

The look in her blue eyes sent warmth and a feeling of pride to his chest, which took him by surprise. Since when had he ever needed or wanted that kind of praise? But coming from Annabelle, it meant something.

"Teamwork, remember? We're all part of it." He drew a long breath, realizing he'd held it for a minute or two there. "Not out of the woods yet, but I think we've got him stable. Definitely a close one. Good thing you were at the hospital, Annabelle. I don't think he'd have made it if we hadn't had a chopper available to get us here fast."

"Guess things happen the way they're meant to sometimes."

Their eyes met for a long, suspended moment. "Maybe sometimes." And other times not. Memories of Gabriel swirled in his head, tangling up with thoughts of Annabelle. Had it been meant to be that they'd work together here? Put the past behind them? Share an embrace that had seemed bigger and more important than a simple kiss should?

Daniel shook off the confusing feelings and focused on repairing the aneurism, making sure the circulation to the abdominal organs and lower extremities was flowing the way it should. He couldn't help but be impressed at the smooth way the team worked together, considering they hadn't been through this kind of emergency surgery before.

After a little more than an hour Daniel got the incision closed and dressed before he finally looked up at his team and pulled down his mask.

"We did it. Jennifer and Karina, you both deserve a gold star for the diagnosis. Annabelle, great work, as usual."

"As usual," she murmured. "Who'd have ever thought those words would come from your lips?"

"Even hardheaded surgeons can learn things, Dr. Richards."

As he said the words, that feeling of confusion filled his head again. Their eyes met once more, held in what felt like a long, suspended moment. He wasn't sure what he was learning, or supposed to be learning. All he knew was that looking into Annabelle's beautiful eyes, spending time with her and talking with her and admiring her goals, felt important. Felt like something he wasn't ready to stop doing, even as the time they spent together here was ticking away.

The sound of squeaking door hinges came from behind them, and Daniel turned to see Eduardo Diaz and Alan Velasco standing just outside the doorway with smiles on both their faces.

"Looks like we missed all the drama. We went to the hotel first, expecting you to be there. But here you are, working, and your receptionist said you're pulling off a miracle."

"Not quite a miracle, but close." He reached to shake both their hands, waiting to feel glad they'd finally arrived. He should. Getting the second clinic up and running and seeing more patients was a good thing. But a sliver of discomfort slid down his spine when he realized he hadn't told Annabelle about his decision to keep her here, working with him. To have Eduardo and Alan go to Huancayo together instead.

What if she didn't want to do that? What if her desire for them to keep a little distance from one another had her insisting she wanted to go to Huancayo now?

"It was an aortic aneurism?" Alan asked. "Never like to see those come in. I've lost a few of those on the table, which we all hate."

"Definitely touch and go," Daniel said. "But we got here in the nick of time, thanks to Karina and Jennifer realizing what his problem was and calling me. And thanks to the hospital in Lima for airlifting us here—if we'd had to drive, he wouldn't be with us right now."

"You were in Lima? Why?"

"Dr. Richards had a meeting there, and I went with her." No need to elaborate. It struck him that Eduardo might want to get involved in her project, since he worked there. The man was single, and Annabelle might even think him good looking. Daniel wanted to be the one to participate in her project, if she'd let him. Not some other Peruvian doc, though he realized he shouldn't think like that. To get her school up and running and have disadvantaged Peruvian kids benefit, too, he should hope she got all kinds of help offered to her.

"Speaking of Lima, do you want to call Dr. Loyola to let him know we're done? Then he can send the helicopter back so they can take the patient to his hospital?" Annabelle asked as she checked the patient's breathing.

Probably because she was as happy about saving this patient as he was, she sent him the dazzling smile she'd knocked him over with the first time they'd worked together in Philadelphia. Before the big catastrophe there. He could see that Alan and Eduardo were looking at her the same way he always had—with interest and appreciation—and his gut tightened.

"Yeah, I will." He didn't particularly want to

introduce the men to Annabelle and the staff, but that was ridiculous, and of course it would be beyond rude not to. "Annabelle, Karina and Jennifer, this is Alan Velasco, anesthesiologist, and Eduardo Diaz, general surgeon."

After hellos all around, Daniel found himself watching how Annabelle walked up to Eduardo and started talking about the Huancayo clinic. At the cute, animated way she told his story about the opossum, joking that she was going to take the cat always hovering outside the hotel to chase any creatures off that might want to sleep there. Even in the middle of calling for the helicopter, he found himself keeping one ear on their conversation.

"Is there some reason you believe a feral cat would be more welcome in a surgical clinic than an opossum, Annabelle?" Eduardo asked, smiling at her in a way that made Daniel grit his teeth.

"I see your point," she said with a faux thoughtful look on her face. "Except Daniel told me they look like rats, and cats are definitely cuter than rats."

"True. But did he tell you about the monkeys? Or the terrifying guinea pigs with nests everywhere, like I had to deal with at the last mission I worked? They're the worst."

Annabelle's eyes sparkled as she laughed. "I think I could handle cute little guinea pigs."

"Not if they were nibbling on your shoes during surgery."

"Have to agree that might be a little distracting."

The glint in Eduardo's eyes as they chuckled together had Daniel quickly moving in to talk about the change of plans. At least, part of them, for now. But there was no way Annabelle was going to Huancayo to work with Eduardo if he had any say about it.

"Annabelle has a meeting in Lima in the morning, and my car is still there. We'll be going back with the patient in the hospital helicopter, driving back tomorrow. Can you both work tomorrow with Karina and Jennifer?" He turned to the nurses. "Okay with you if you spend some time finding patients that need general surgery? We'll delay the cardiac patients until I get back."

"Sure, that's fine," Eduardo said. "Then Annabelle and I will head to Huancayo."

Which was not Daniel's plan anymore.

"Karina, please get the patient ready to transfer to the helicopter, so he's ready when it gets here." he said. "Annabelle, I have your bag here. Need anything else before we go back?"

All the amusement from her banter with Eduardo was gone as her eyes met his, almost searchingly. As he wondered what she was looking for, or what she might be seeing, she spoke.

"No. I'm ready. I appreciate you taking the extra time away from surgeries, but with Huancayo open we'll be able to see a lot of people for different kinds of treatments. So don't worry."

"Not worrying," he said gruffly.

Not about that anyway. But about how Annabelle was going to take his about-face, wanting her to stay in Ayllu to work with him? He wasn't at all sure how she was going to feel about that.

With Karina focused on the patient and the rest of them off to the hotel, he steered Annabelle to a quiet corner of the building.

"I need to talk to you about something."

Serious blue eyes met his. "I thought it seemed like there was something on your mind other than our patient. Other than going back to Lima."

Funny how they'd gotten to know one another so well in such a short time. Even after all the animosity between them. Or was that part of the reason he felt so strangely close to her? Maybe the high emotions of all kinds flaring between the two of them had made them hyperaware of each other in a way he never had with anyone.

"I've changed my mind about something."

"You don't want me to stay at your grand-parents' anymore? If not, I understand. There's plenty of time for me to find a hotel." Her expression didn't change, but he thought maybe her eyes seemed a little melancholy.

"No. They'll love meeting you, and I think you'll like them, too. It's about Huancayo."

"Huancayo?"

"Yes." He grasped her shoulders and brought her closer so Karina couldn't possibly hear. "When we cleared the air about what happened five years ago, I told you that I know you're very good at your job. And you proved that again today during a tricky, critical surgery. Because I'm the autocratic, stern perfectionist you've accused me of being, I don't want you to go to Huancayo. I want you to stay and work with me."

"You…you want me to stay?"

"Yes. Will you? Eduardo and Alan can work together at the other clinic. I need the best, and the best is you."

Her pretty lips parted as she stared at him. "You brought Alan here because you thought he was the best."

"He's good. You're better." In so many ways. The pleasure of seeing her in the OR with him, working with her even if it was only for another week, made his heart feel full, even as he hated the thought of saying goodbye so soon.

"I don't know what to say. I was mentally ready to go to the other clinic."

"How about getting mentally ready to work with me just a little longer? Please?"

Finally, a smile formed on her beautiful lips. "That might require a double dose of yoga poses, Dr. Ferrera. But, yes, since, astonishingly, you asked nicely, I'll work here with you for the rest of the mission."

"Thank you." He extended his hand for a handshake to prevent himself from leaning in and giving her a kiss.

Annabelle thought Daniel might stay in the back of the chopper the entire flight to monitor their patient, but soon the empty spot next to her was filled with his large body. His warm hand reached for hers and held it tight.

"He's doing well. Vital signs are all stable, though the EMT is going to keep an eye on him to make sure that doesn't change."

"Good to hear." She looked down at their entwined fingers. Part of her thought she shouldn't let that happen, but it was just for reassurance, right? Because he knew she wasn't crazy about

flying in the chopper and was just being a gentleman.

A gentleman who had held her hand for a lot
longer than was necessary, much longer than a
professional handshake should normally last. A
gentleman she caught giving her the kinds of
glances that made her heart speed up and made
her feel a little breathless.

Resisting getting involved with this man wasn't
going to be easy, but it was only for another week,
right? She could do it.

Darkness had fallen on Lima by the time they
landed on the helipad of the hospital, and Annabelle felt a tinge of regret that they were too
late to enjoy the view of the ocean from Miraflores that she'd heard was amazing. But, of
course, she wasn't here for sightseeing. Not to
spend time with Daniel as though they were on
a date or something. She was here for business,
nothing more.

Daniel's car was parked in the hospital garage,
and in no time they were driving through the city

towards his grandparents' place. Tall high-rises were built all along the top of the cliffs, shining and glittering in golden light. Annabelle couldn't remember seeing city lights that seemed so welcoming, and she gasped when she finally saw the ocean waves beyond the steep cliff, their white-caps lit by moonlight.

"This is so beautiful. I've never seen any part of the city at night, and definitely not this part, with so many buildings practically on the edge of the cliff, with the beautiful ocean farther on. Are those apartment buildings, or offices, or what?"

"A combination of both, along with hotels. For people who can afford it, Miraflores is a desirable place to live and a popular tourist site, too. Not quite up there with Machu Picchu," he said, flashing her a smile so devastatingly appealing she found herself staring at his mouth and remembering their kiss. "But plenty of people stay here and take a train or bus to the ruins."

"One of these trips I need to see Machu Picchu. Whenever I get back from here, people sometimes ask me about it and I always feel a little foolish that I haven't made the effort to go. But there's only so much vacation time, and too many patients who need surgery." She looked at his profile, knowing he understood, since he donated his time to their care, too.

"Yes. But once in a while you have to do something for fun that's relaxing and educational and amazing all at the same time, which visiting the ruins is. A person risks burnout working all the time."

"Maybe." She was tempted to say more, even though few people really understood how she felt about her life and its purpose. The reason she'd survived, when she easily might not have. But, somehow, she felt like Daniel would understand.

"It's hard to just relax and do frivolous things when there's such a huge need here and at home."

"At home? In Chicago?" When he glanced at her, his eyebrows were raised over his questioning eyes. Part of her regretted bringing up the subject of need and poverty. But, of course, there was no way he'd find out she'd been one of the neediest kids around. The kind she tried to help now.

"Yeah. There are so many underprivileged kids in Chicago, and obviously lots of other places, who just need to spend time with someone who cares about them. One person who just might completely change a child's life if they learn to have a little confidence in themselves, to believe there's more to life than the poverty they were born into."

Realizing he might think the passionate tone in her voice was a bit much, she swallowed and took it down a notch. "And here? You know it's even more than that. If we're here to help, or not here, it can truly be a question of living or dying."

"Yes. That's why we're on this trip." he said quietly. "But one person can't change the world, Annabelle. And each one of us has to take care of ourselves, too, or we won't be of any use to the people you're talking about."

"You're wrong," she whispered. "One person can make all the difference. Just one person who cares to. But anyway…" Time to move away from the heavy subject she'd started, before he asked any more questions she didn't want to answer. "Tell me about your grandparents and your family. Were you born here or in the States?"

"I was born here. Moved to the US when I was ten. At that time political violence became too much for my parents to want to stay here, with the government corrupt and terrorist groups killing people in outlying villages. I never saw any of it, I only know this from reading about the history and talking to my family. Thankfully, Peru is a functioning democracy again and a safe place to live."

"Wow, as I said before I'd heard about how bad it was. I can't believe you actually had to leave because of it, though."

"That wasn't the only reason." His lips seemed to thin, and he pointed to the gorgeous buildings they were approaching. "My grandparents live in that building, right there, with lights all around the top. We'll be there in just a few minutes."

Now, that was a clear change of subject, and

since Annabelle didn't want him asking too many questions about her childhood either, she made idle conversation about the city and the lovely ocean waves she could see beyond the cliff instead.

Traffic was fairly heavy, considering it was 8:00 p.m., with numerous pedestrians on the sidewalks, going into restaurants and various shops. They circled a roundabout with a beautiful fountain in the center before Daniel turned the car onto a side street, then into a large parking garage.

"I have an idea," he said as he nosed the vehicle into a numbered spot she assumed belonged to his grandparents. "We'll meet my grandparents then go out for a light dinner and nightcap. I have a few favorite spots overlooking the water I think you'd enjoy."

"Is this because you know I like to eat?"

He laughed, and it struck her again how much younger he seemed, how relaxed compared to the intensity he brought to the OR. "I like to eat too, remember? Plus, I want you to experience some real Peruvian food. That stuff they fix in the hotel in Ayllu is made for what they think is American and European tastes and pretty awful, in my opinion."

"I'd love to try authentic Peruvian food while looking out over the ocean." And admire Daniel's sculpted face. Get to enjoy that smile and laugh of his that was such a surprise. The kind of surprise that curled up inside her belly and made her feel strangely warm and oddly happy.

Which meant she might be in trouble with a capital *T*.

The elevator opened with a soft swish, and when Daniel punched in a code then hit the button to the top floor, she stared at him, surprised. "Your grandparents live on the top floor?"

"My grandmother likes flowers, so a rooftop garden was one of her priorities when they were looking for a place here." The door pinged open and he placed his hand on her back to usher her out.

"Which apartment is it?" she asked, feeling a

little confused that there seemed to be only one large double door in the hallway.

"They own the whole floor."

CHAPTER EIGHT

"THE WHOLE FLOOR?" Annabelle squeaked. "Daniel, you didn't tell me…"

"Why are you looking like that?" He tipped his head to look at her, obviously perplexed at whatever stunned expression she had on her face. Probably his rich Peruvian friends and doctor pals were all used to affluence.

"I'm just…surprised. A penthouse suite." She nearly laughed nervously but decided it was good she knew this now. Knew even more than she had before that the silly daydreams popping unbidden into her head about Daniel definitely had to be dashed, and pronto. Telling herself there'd be no more kissing with him had been a good decision, and she had to stick with it.

"Only the best," he said lightly, smiling at her again. His hand moved from her back to grasp her elbow, leaning down to speak close to her ear as they approached the door and rang the bell. "They're actually wonderful people, I promise."

Wonderful people with boatloads of money who would doubtless be less than enthused about their grandson dating someone below their social class. Not that she and Daniel were dating or anything.

"Daniel!" An elegant woman in a beautiful red pantsuit opened the door and enfolded him in an embrace as she kissed both cheeks. "We were so happy to get your call! Why didn't you tell us you were in Peru? It's lucky we aren't in Paracas, as we just came here a few days ago so your grandfather could attend to some business."

"I'm sorry, I should have let you know sooner." He returned her kiss, then stepped to give a robust hug to the equally elegant, gray-haired man beaming behind her. "It's great to see you, Abuelo. You're looking fit, as always."

"And you are a sight for sore eyes, Daniel. We were just talking about visiting the States soon to see you and your parents, but here you are."

Both men stood grinning at one another until Daniel turned his smile toward Annabelle.

"Abuela, Abuelo, this is Dr. Annabelle Richards. Annabelle, my grandparents Sebastian and Cynthia de la Piedra Ferrera."

De la Piedra Ferrera? If that didn't sound like Peruvian aristocracy, nothing did. Tempted to wipe her hands down her dress, Annabelle hoped they weren't too sweaty as she reached to shake their hands. "It's nice to meet you. Thank you for allowing me to stay here. Daniel may have told you I have a meeting early in the morning and he was kind enough to offer, if that's okay with you."

"Of course! We are delighted to have a friend and coworker of Daniel's here," Cynthia said with what looked like a genuine smile. But, of course, they probably thought she was his peer, since she was a doctor. She could only hope they wouldn't find out how wrong they were about that.

Another thing that proved how upper-crust they were compared to her lowliness? Their English. It was so impeccable, with only the slightest accent, that she immediately vowed again to herself to learn more Spanish, and not just learn it but speak it as beautifully as they did.

If her stomach hadn't felt a little queasy before, it would have gotten that way when she entered the apartment. The obviously expensive modern furniture, artwork and accessories in the large room were stunning enough. Yet they were completely overshadowed by the incredible views out the ceiling-to-floor windows that made up the entire back of the room.

Never in her life had she been in such a place. Had barely even known homes like this existed, except in fancy magazines featuring glossy photos of the rich and famous.

"Come look at the view," Daniel said. He reached for her hand, probably because he sensed she felt frozen in place, and tugged her gently toward the windows. His eyes met hers, serious now, and she could only imagine what he was seeing in her eyes and on her face. "It's pretty, isn't it?"

Since he had to know it was so beyond pretty

there wasn't a word for it, she just silently nodded as she stared outside. White-capped waves steadily moved toward the shore, and a lighthouse in the distance blinked. In every direction she looked there were more glass buildings and lights. Below, cars that looked tiny from up here moved all directions, their headlamps competing with the city lights. And to top it all off, a bright moon hung in the dark sky, as though she was standing on some stage set designed to create a place of utter tranquility and beauty.

"It's…incredible," she finally managed to say. "I can't imagine what it's like to get to look out on this kind of view every day."

"We enjoy it," Sebastian said, which struck Annabelle as either an incredible understatement or perhaps the simple words really did express how he felt. Casual about it, because he'd enjoyed spectacular settings his whole life. "And also enjoy sharing it with friends and family whenever we can."

"How about a drink? Are you hungry?" Cynthia asked.

Daniel's strong hand gave hers a squeeze as he smiled down at her. "Annabelle hasn't spent any time in Lima, so I thought we'd walk around just a bit, have a bite to eat somewhere, then come back."

"Lima is a beautiful city, and of course we're partial to Miraflores, so by all means go enjoy it a bit," Cynthia said. "We'll see you when you get back or, if you stay out late, in the morning."

"We won't be late. Annabelle needs to be at her meeting early. We'll be back soon."

More hugs and kisses and smiles between the three of them left Annabelle's throat thick with longing. What must it be like to have a family like theirs? A family who loved being together and obviously supported one another. A family with the means and desire to travel long distances just to spend time together.

Having been more or less alone her whole life, even when her mother had been around, she just couldn't imagine it. Had never allowed herself to think much about what that would feel like.

Was there any way she could figure out what

a real family was like, and set having one as another goal for her future? Maybe someday she could see if there was a mentor for that, too.

Back in the elevator after their goodbyes, Annabelle stood silently next to Daniel, having no idea what to say.

"I can tell you're uncomfortable," Daniel said, and she couldn't decide if she was glad he knew or if she wished he was oblivious. "Why?"

"I just… I don't belong in a place like this."

"What do you mean?"

"I'm… Never mind." She blew out a breath, knowing she was being ridiculous. It wasn't as though she and Daniel were dating, and his grandparents would look down on her as a possible future mate or something. The two of them had just recently become somewhat friends, right? "I was just surprised at your family's station in life. Is your name really Daniel de la Piedra Ferrera?"

"Yes, from our family estate in Paracas. But for obvious reasons I don't use all of it," he said with his lips curving slightly.

"Your family estate. I mean, that's really nice for you to have that. To come from that."

His smile disappeared. "I come from wealth, yes. But that doesn't define who I am, and not coming from money and privilege doesn't define you either."

She felt herself flush in embarrassment. "How do you know I don't?" But of course he knew. Anyone could tell she didn't have anywhere near the sophistication of a man like Daniel de la Piedra Ferrera.

"Only because you seem intimidated by it. But here's what you need to think about. The people who are to be most admired are those who've worked hard to accomplish something." The elevator doors opened, and he tugged her hand as he strode out of the garage to the lights of the city streets. "My grandparents came from money, but have also worked hard in the family businesses. Some of my family's friends who inherited money do nothing but play. Don't try to do a damn thing for those who would use their help. I'm not like that, and you're not like that."

She didn't answer, because it wasn't the same thing at all. He grasped her shoulders and turned her toward him, his dark eyes almost stormy as he looked down at her.

"You worked hard to go to medical school, and so did I. We work at clinics in other countries to help those who don't have the advantage of being born in the United States." His warm fingers slipped beneath her chin and lifted her gaze to his. "You and I are more alike than we are different, Annabelle Richards. Something I've come to see more than I understood even yesterday."

He lowered his head and touched his mouth to hers, so sweetly and softly it made her chest squeeze and prickles skitter across her skin. For long moments the kiss was light, a soothing caress designed to make her forget her worries, she knew. And it worked, because every apprehension, every feeling of utter inadequacy slipped away beneath the barrage of sensation his warm lips made her feel.

Weak and wired, dizzy and alive. Her hands slipped up his firm chest to wrap around his neck and at the same time his arms curved around her back, pressing her body to his, torso to torso, hip to hip, thigh to thigh.

"Annabelle," he whispered against her lips before delving deeper. She quivered in her shoes, everything forgotten but the taste of him and the feel of him.

The sound of nearby laughter finally seeped through the sensual fog in her brain, and she managed to pull away, blinking at the sexual heat swirling around them. A throng of people, including a few giggling children, walked by, and hot color rushed into her cheeks as she realized they'd been making out in a very public place. The man was clearly making her lose her mind.

"Kissing you here probably isn't the best idea," he said with a small smile on the lips that had just made her swoon. "Let's get that food and drink, hmm?"

"Um, good idea."

The big hand grasping hers somehow felt normal and right, even though she told herself she should pull it loose. Take a step sideways so she couldn't feel all that masculine heat radiating from him as they walked along a pedestrian walkway by the cliff.

Looking out over the ocean, listening to the distant sound of the surf and the happy voices nearby, she couldn't remember ever feeling so strangely content at the same time she still felt distinctly out of place.

Daniel didn't know the full truth about her past, but maybe he was right. Maybe it was time she set aside her insecurities about her childhood. Maybe it really was time to act like the adult she was, the person she'd worked so hard to become, and stop worrying about social classes and who belonged where and why.

"Here's my favorite restaurant, where we can sit outside and look out over the sea while you enjoy a few Peruvian delicacies," Daniel said, steering her to a table where a waitress came over with menus. "What's your tipple?"

"I don't drink. Alcohol, I mean. But if there's some special Peruvian beverage you want me to try, I'm willing to make an exception."

"Believe it or not, the most famous drink native to Peru is nonalcoholic. It's called *chicha morada*, and goes back to before the Incan Empire."

"Never thought I'd be offered a drink that goes back to the Incan Empire. What's in it?"

"You can't be turned off by the fact that it's made from boiled purple corn." He gave her a grin. "It's mixed with pineapple and some spices, I think maybe cinnamon and cloves. Sounds strange to an American, I know, but I think you'd like it."

"Sounds a little weird." She grinned back. "But who am I to turn down a boiled corn drink?"

"I suspected you were adventurous." He dropped a kiss onto her forehead and she found herself leaning into it, even as she knew she should tell him to cut it out. "I also have a few suggestions about food."

"That's handy, because I can't read Spanish. At least, not as much as I should." She tucked her menu beneath his. "Which I've decided has to change. I come to Central and South America enough that I need to become more fluent, and it would help me talk to Hispanic patients at home, too."

"I'll help you practice some if you like."

She nearly opened her mouth to say yes, until their eyes met and she realized that couldn't happen. Soon she'd be returning to Chicago and he to Philadelphia and they'd probably never see one another again.

Even as it was clear he was thinking exactly what she was thinking, that expected flash of heat was right there between them again. Her stomach twisted and her breath backed up in her lungs and the air felt thick with a sexual awareness that suddenly seemed to surround them whenever they were close together.

The moment seemed to last forever, until she became aware that the waitress was standing in front of them and talking. Daniel redirected his attention to the menu and either asked the woman questions or answered hers. Annabelle had no idea which one it was, but it didn't matter because she'd long ago realized she loved listening to the lovely lilt of the language spoken in his deep bass. Loved watching his sculpted lips move, and as she did so loved the memories the action evoked of their kisses and how they had made her feel, leaving her breathless all over again.

Yep. Trouble with a capital *T*, but at least it wouldn't last for long.

Daniel handed the menus to the waitress then turned to Annabelle with a smile. "Hope it's okay that I went ahead and ordered. I figured we could talk forever about what you might like, or I could just get things I like and let you try them."

"You already know I like just about everything. Probably, though, I should stop practically licking my plate at every meal." She knew that having had so little food for so many years had left her unconsciously feeling like she had to take advantage of every meal while it was in front of her. Now that she was not in a position where she'd ever go hungry she needed to fix that, but it seemed somehow deeply ingrained.

"Which is a good thing, as far as I'm concerned." He leaned down to kiss her gently on the lips, and she couldn't make herself pull away. "I'm just now realizing that you are down on yourself sometimes. How is that possible, when you are smart and educated and so beautiful on top of all that?"

His words warmed her heart, though she felt embarrassed. If he knew all the truth about her, he wouldn't be so complimentary. "Maybe because certain surgeons have doubted my abilities in the past?" she said lightly, wanting to move the subject to a place they could smile about during the time they had together here.

"I'm not even going to comment on that." He bumped his shoulder into hers. "So. Food. I ordered ceviche and tiradito, which is a fish prepared a bit like the ceviche. We have the best seafood in the world here, as far as I'm concerned, and I think you'll like it. Then a dish that has stir-fried beef with fried potatoes, onions, tomato and spicy peppers, and chicken in a cream sauce made with a special Peruvian chili. We'll see if we want more after we've eaten all that."

"More? I know you've seen me wolf down all

my food, but I'm sure all that will fill me up. Sounds absolutely delicious."

"We'll see. I want you to enjoy good food while you're here." He grinned down at her. "I—"

The abrupt way he stopped in midsentence, his expression flattening into something worrying that she couldn't quite define, had her leaning close to him and putting her hand on his arm. "What is it? Is something wrong?"

He pressed his hand to his chest and shook his head without answering. A grimace now twisted his lips, and her heart started beating hard because it was clear that something was going on with him, and also clear he didn't want to share it.

"Daniel, if you're ill you need to tell me." She reached for his wrist and he tried to pull it from her grasp, but his effort was weak. She stared at her watch as she felt his pulse, and alarm skittered across her skin when she saw it was shockingly fast.

CHAPTER NINE

"YOUR PULSE IS ONE-FORTY, and completely irregular," Annabelle said, dismayed at the way his skin seemed stretched tight across his face in obvious discomfort. "You're in A-fib, aren't you?"

"It's…something that happens sometimes."

"Why?"

He stared out at the ocean and didn't answer, which ratcheted up her sense of alarm.

"Do you have meds for it?"

He nodded. "In my bag. At the apartment."

"I'll go get it."

She went to stand, but he grabbed her arm. "Just…wait a few minutes. Sometimes it doesn't last long."

Part of her wanted to sprint to his grandparents' apartment anyway. But it was obvious this wasn't a new experience for him, and knew how he was feeling. After long minutes had ticked by and the first course of foods were served, her fear escalated, as she could easily see he wasn't feeling any better at all.

"Listen, there's no point in toughing this out. Tell the waitress to bring the check while I get your medicine."

"I…think I can walk there." He tossed a wad of cash on the table and started to stand up, but dropped right back into the seat, his head swaying as though he couldn't keep it upright.

"Daniel!" She grasped his face in her hands and he blinked up at her, looking confused. "You're feeling faint, aren't you? Blood pressure must be dropping. I'm going to have them call an ambulance."

"No." His fingers wrapped around her wrist. "No hospital. I'll be fine. I just need the meds. In a black leather bag in my duffle."

She nodded, then jumped up and ran toward his grandparents' building, her heart hammering hard in her chest. Was she doing the right thing? Should she do as he wanted, or just ignore him and get an emergency medical team with equipment there as soon as possible?

God, she didn't know, but maybe his grandparents could give her some insight. They could call for an ambulance if they felt that should happen.

Out of breath, she finally arrived at the elevator. A small, frantic sob left her lips as she stared at the keypad, remembering he'd had to punch in a security code to get it to open. Why hadn't she thought to just get their phone number from Daniel and call first? Even have them bring the meds?

Too late for that. She closed her eyes, willing herself to remember. Visual details were something she was good at, and as she pictured his finger punching in the number, she opened her eyes and prayed she was right.

Relief weakened her knees as the doors slid open and she made her way to the top floor, praying the elevator didn't stop on any other floors along the way. Her repeated hard banging on their door had Sebastian opening it with a perplexed frown, with Cynthia approaching the door behind him.

"Mr. Ferrera! Daniel is ill. His heart is in arrhythmia, and he's feeling faint. He didn't want me to call an ambulance. Said he has medicine here, in his bag. Do you know about this? Should we call for help or get the meds to him?"

A worried cry left Cynthia's lips as Sebastian quickly turned to practically run down a hallway at the end of the large room. "I'll get the medicine from his bag. Where is he?"

"At a restaurant about two blocks away. I… I don't remember the name of it but I know where it is."

"We'll come with you." Cynthia said, clutching her hands together. "Hurry, Sebastian!"

"He said this happens sometimes. Why?"

"Daniel was born with a heart defect, a hole in the heart. Ventricle septal defect. I'm sure you know of it."

Sebastian returned with a bottle in his hand and the three of them hurried to the elevator.

"Yes. It was never repaired?"

"It was small, as was his brother's. Their hearts seemed to be functioning normally, so doctors simply kept an eye on them."

"Brother?" Annabelle stared at Cynthia as they strode quickly down the street toward the restaurant. "He has a brother with the same condition?"

Her face clouded as she shook her head. "He died. He was Daniel's twin. I don't think he ever got over it. Daniel kept on living with just these little scares now and then, but his brother died."

"Oh, my God, that's terrible." Annabelle didn't know what it was like to have a sibling or to lose one, had never had any family members to be close to. Her heart ached for Daniel losing his brother, and not just a brother but a twin. She'd seen so many grieving family members over the years she'd been in medicine, and knew the devastation of that kind of loss.

"It was," Sebastian said grimly. "Our Daniel decided to become a cardiac surgeon because of it, instead of going into the family businesses as expected. It's scary when he gets ill like this, because you never know, do you? He's always been fine so far, but we thought that about Gabriel, too."

Gabriel must be his brother's name. Annabelle wanted to ask what had happened him, why exactly he'd died, but they were almost at the restaurant and helping Daniel was the urgent priority.

"Over here."

Daniel was sitting in the same spot with his face in his hands as they approached. Both grandparents started speaking to him in Spanish, and he lifted his head to look at them. Annabelle had assumed she'd take over administering the medicine, but it was obvious this drill wasn't new to Sebastian and Cynthia. They sat on either side of him, one grasping his hand to put the pills into his palm, the other holding up a glass of water.

Annabelle knew that, often, the arrhythmia would go away almost immediately after administering meds, and at other times it took a while before the patient felt better. She wanted to ask Daniel questions about how he was feeling but, with his grandparents there to care for him, felt uncomfortable sticking her nose in, doctor or not.

Standing there, watching, she tried to wrap her mind around what the Ferreras had just told her. Daniel had a heart defect. His twin brother had died from it, and he'd become a cardiac surgeon because of it. Could that be part of why he was even more intense in the OR than most surgeons she knew? Utterly intolerant of the slightest mistake? Had his brother died because of an error on someone's part?

Minutes ticked by as she watched Daniel blink, nod at his grandparents, then slowly turn his head to look up at her. "I'm sorry, Annabelle."

Her throat closed. "Sorry? For what? For not feeling well during an A-fib attack? There are some things you should apologize to me for, but that's not one of them."

He actually managed to smile at her, and the sweetness of it pinched her heart. "True. But I was apologizing for you not getting to enjoy all the food I promised you'd like."

"Well, I am pretty upset about that." She

reached for his wrist and was glad he didn't object. "Let me check your pulse."

"I can tell it's about back to normal now."

"Let me check anyway, if only to reassure your grandparents and me." Just feeling his pulse for a second eased the tightness in her own chest, but she stared at her watch for a full minute to make sure, finally huffing out the breath she'd been holding in her lungs. "Okay. All good. About ninety. How are you feeling?"

"Other than embarrassed?" His lips twisted as his brown eyes met hers. "Slightly worn out but fine."

"Let's have this food packed up and we'll take it home," Cynthia said, moving away to speak with someone in the restaurant.

The man felt embarrassed? Did he somehow think his heart problem, and tonight's event, made him seem weak or less manly? That couldn't have been further from the truth. The man was a tower of strength and power when it came to his personality, drive and presence in the OR and out of it, and when the time was right she'd somehow make sure he knew that.

The walk back to the apartment was mostly silent, as no one seemed to feel like talking now that the worst was over and Daniel obviously felt reasonably all right. He walked with a normal gait, his posture tall and proud. Cynthia insisted on serving the cold ceviche and warming the rest of the food, even though it was obvious Daniel didn't really feel like eating and Annabelle's normally robust appetite was definitely gone.

But they ate anyway, his grandparents very focused on making smiling small talk, even though their expressions were strained. She wondered if it might be because they knew Daniel wasn't happy to have this episode happen in front of a woman he'd brought to their home. Pretending everything was fine and normal just wasn't possible, as far as Annabelle was concerned, but she went along with it, forcing herself to come up with chit-chat and make comments over the food.

In truth, she could barely taste it, looking at Daniel's chiseled features that looked so remarkably normal now, in stark contrast to his drawn pallor in the restaurant, which had scared her to death. Her heart squeezed at the thought of how much pain he'd gone through over his brother's death, and she didn't have to be a psychologist to know that living with a heart defect himself had to color everything he did.

"Thank you for suggesting we bring the food here, Abuela. I was worried Annabelle would go hungry."

His words were meant to be light and joking, she knew, except he had no idea how many times she actually had.

"I enjoyed it, but you know I always do," she said, trying to match his tone. Problem was, she felt all small-talked out. Was it late enough that she could escape to her room? So Daniel could rest, too?

"I think I'd like to go to bed now, even though it's not very late. My meeting is early, and I need to go over some paperwork."

"Of course. We shall see you in the morning." Cynthia embraced her, and Annabelle was surprised how nice it felt, even though she barely knew the woman. What would it be like to have a mother or grandmother to hug? Pretty nice, if she was as lovely as Cynthia.

"I think I will too," Daniel said. "We'll catch up more tomorrow."

Annabelle wistfully watched the three of them hug again, their love for one another obvious on their faces. She turned away, refusing to give herself a pity party on how different her own experiences were. Life might have been tough, but it had shaped her into who she was. A person who was committed to make a difference to help kids being dragged up the way she'd been, instead of raised with care and given every opportunity to learn who they might want to become.

Cynthia led them down a plush, carpeted hallway lined with interesting artwork that looked nothing like the cheap posters Annabelle had hanging on the walls of her own apartment.

"Daniel, you know where your room is. Annabelle, you're sleeping in here," Cynthia said, stopping in front of a doorway open to a beautiful room decorated in muted shades of green. "I hope everything you need is here, but please don't hesitate to let us know if something is missing. Sebastian and I will be up for several more hours, and if you need something in the middle of the night, just dial number one on the phone intercom. Our room is off the other wing."

To think that the wealthy woman of the house offered to be on call in the middle of the night, like she was staying in a hotel, calling the reception desk, boggled Annabelle's mind. "I'm sure everything will be perfect. Thank you again for letting me stay with you."

The hallway seemed to close in on them when the older woman disappeared around the corner, leaving Daniel and Annabelle alone. He stood next to her, his eyes on hers. Serious now. Somber even. She opened her mouth, trying to think of all the things she wanted to say and how to say them, when he took a step closer and touched his finger to her lips.

"Shh. I know all the stuff you're thinking of saying, all the pity that you feel for me, how miserable and sad, and I want you to know, right now, that it's completely misplaced. It is what it is, and it doesn't keep me from living my life the way I want to. It's over with, for the moment, and I'm fine."

"You have no idea what I've wanted to say to you. Because it sure isn't feeling sad for poor you having to live with a problem that derails you once in a while."

Just as she'd suspected before, the last thing he'd ever want was for someone to think he was weak or pitiable, and since she didn't, it was easy to get tough with him about that.

His eyebrows rose, and she closed the gap between them, poking a fingertip into his chest just as she'd done a few times before when she'd been angry with him. "There's that god complex again, thinking you know everything about everyone. Having a bit of a leaky valve, or aortic stenosis, or whatever it is you're dealing with doesn't have a thing to do with your strength as a human being, both physically and mentally."

"I wish you'd stop accusing me of having a god

complex," he murmured, grasping her hand in his and holding it against his sternum.

"Oh, you do. No doubt about that. But along with that annoying negative, a lot of positives make up the man you are. I've worked with more surgeons than I can count, and while you're the toughest one in the OR, you have sweetness in that imperfect heart of yours for the ill and vulnerable children we've taken care of. And now that I have a better idea why you're so rough on everyone on a surgical team, I respect you even more."

"Yeah?" His lips began to curve. "So you're not going to fall all over me and weep and say how sorry you feel for me? And here I was dreading that, but instead you're insulting me."

"Aren't you hearing my compliments?"

"Yes." He leaned down to whisper the words against her mouth. "Thank you. Now it's my turn to tell you how wonderful you are in every way."

"That is beyond not true, as you well know. I—"

"Must you argue against every compliment you

get?" he interrupted. "Just say thank you, the way I did."

She looked up at him, thinking that he was right, and that it had to be annoying to anyone who said something nice to her.

"All right. Thank you. Now back to you, and no arguing from your end either. Even though you're feeling okay now, you should lie down and rest. Your heart going out of rhythm stresses every part of your body for a bit, as you well know."

"I'll take your good doctor's advice, under one condition."

"What condition?"

"That you lie down with me."

Oh, how she wanted to. Thinking of his long body pressed up against hers made her feel a little breathless, at the same time a warm tenderness swept over her. Had she ever had a man just want to lie down with her? Talk? Share about themselves?

Maybe he had another agenda, or maybe he didn't. And she wasn't about to share everything about herself. But it would give her a chance to ask him about his brother, to see if he wanted to talk about it to someone. And if he didn't, just quietly holding him close would be the nicest thing she'd done in a long, long time.

"I'd like that very much."

He reached for her hand and led her into the room, shutting the door behind them. A startled gasp left her lips when he picked her up and deposited her on the bed, following to lie right next to her.

"Picking me up isn't part of your resting plan. I'm no featherweight."

"And I'm no weakling. Didn't you say my problems shouldn't affect my strength?"

"I meant your inner strength, and you know it."

He hauled her closer, cocooning her against his side. The intimate feeling of resting her head against his muscled shoulder and chest crept into her heart, filling her with yet more confusing feelings. Wonderful feelings. Sad feelings.

Daniel was so far out of her league it was like they were from different solar systems. But maybe she was ready to change her mind about a fling with him. Knowing that was all there could be between them made it seem more tempting. Even inevitable. She knew she couldn't let herself fantasize about anything past one or two days together. That would just be a pipe dream, like ones she'd had so often as a child. Dreams of wanting things she could never have, and never would.

As Jennifer had said, being with Daniel for just a short time wouldn't make her anything like her mother. Being held in his warm arms now, she knew that a short fling with a man like him would be an experience she'd never forget.

The way his lips touched her forehead, the feeling of his hand stroking her hair, sliding up and down her arm, added to the sweet sense of intimacy they shared as they lay in the darkness of the room.

She wondered if Daniel felt the same intimacy. And if he did, perhaps it would make him feel like he could talk about his heart condition. About his brother. If he'd want to unburden himself in some way about that terrible event, or about tonight's arrhythmia episode in a public place that would feel uncomfortable and even embarrassing to anyone.

She wouldn't push. But she was going to ask.

"Tell me about your brother," she said quietly.

"My brother?"

Her chest tightened at his tone and the way the large hand resting on her stomach curled a little into her flesh. But being surprised at the question didn't necessarily mean he didn't want to talk about it.

"Your grandmother told me you had a twin brother who'd also been born with a congenital heart defect. And that he died. That must have been unbelievably horrible for your whole family."

The silence that followed made her wish she'd kept her mouth shut. Why couldn't she just have enjoyed the comfort of lying there with him, instead of ruining it? Her heart lodged in her throat as she tried to figure out what to say next. Or maybe she should just give him a sweet kiss goodnight and head to her own room. Just as she'd decided to do both those things, he spoke.

"Gabriel and I were born three minutes apart, with me coming first. I always liked to call him my baby brother, because it irritated him no end." Through the near darkness, a shadow of a smile touched his lips. "He'd respond that I might be the older brother but he was the better-looking, smarter, more charming brother."

"Sounds like he had a wonderful sense of humor. That you were close."

"Yeah, we were. Played all kinds of sports together, competed for good grades in school, played pranks on our nanny and our friends."

"So what heart condition were you both born with that you could have pretty normal childhoods?"

"I'm told we were about six months old when our doctor here realized we had heart murmurs, and after tests both of us were diagnosed with VSD. We were regularly monitored, but the valve leakage for both of us was minor. With the aorta growing as a child grows, surgery wasn't the best option when we could simply wait and see."

Annabelle stayed silent, hoping he'd keep talking, and when he finally did felt so glad she'd risked asking him.

"As I told you before, we moved to the States when we were about ten, and saw new doctors there. Obviously very good doctors, I'm not claiming they weren't. Our EKGs were normal, blood flow was normal. We were happy, healthy kids. Until we were seventeen, and the doctor thought Gabriel's murmur was getting worse. Surface echocardiogram showed the hole in Gabriel's heart had enlarged and needed to be repaired."

Oh, no. Annabelle's heart clutched, because she had a feeling she knew what was coming next. "And it didn't go well."

He stirred, lifting his hand to run it down his face before he nodded. "The most experienced cardiac surgeon was on vacation, so a different guy did the surgery. Everyone assured us he was top-notch, too. But a few hours after the operation Gabriel's blood pressure dropped, his oxygen level was low and he was struggling to breathe. Everyone figured he must have post-op bleeding."

Obviously, this story didn't have a happy ending, and she waited to hear the worst.

"They rushed him back to the OR and opened the incision to find fluid built up in his pericardial sac. He ended up in cardiac arrest and stopped breathing. And they couldn't bring him back." The tortured look in his eyes broke her heart. "He never got to see his eighteenth birthday, which was a week after he died."

"Oh, Daniel," she whispered, lifting her hand to cup his cheek. "I'm so sorry. And you had to have that birthday without him. I can't imagine how that felt."

His eyes closed, and she knew he was feeling the pain all over again. She pulled him closer, and this time she was the one who pressed her lips against his forehead. He leaned toward her, and she moved her cheek to rub it softly against his in a caress.

"It was bad. The shock about killed us, too." He pulled her even closer, breast to chest. "My parents were a mess, and I was a typical youth, self-absorbed and unable to process it. I buried the pain for a long time. Maybe I still do."

"And you became a cardiac surgeon because of it. As a way to deal with it." Even if his grandmother hadn't told her that, it would have been easy to guess.

"I wanted to make sure that no one ever died the way Gabriel did. That no family would have to go through what we went through." He pulled back to look at her somberly. "But, of course, after medical school I realized that was impossible. You know that as well as I do. People die, and the people who love them suffer. But I've made it my mission to keep that from happening to the best of my ability."

"And you've succeeded." She cupped his face in her palm. "You're beyond skilled, and demand the best from everyone you work with. I get why you had me booted out."

He shook his head, his lips brushing against her

palm. "I should have checked to see your track record, your ratings from other doctors, before pushing for that."

"No. It was my responsibility to keep close tabs on the resident. I deserved what I got."

"Not sure about that now." He lifted his face to hers to give her a soft kiss. "But if this means you're not angry with me anymore, I'll take it."

"Considering I'm curled up next to you in bed, I think it's a safe bet to say I'm not angry at you anymore."

A smile curved his lips and the sadness in his eyes began to lift. "I'm not a betting man, but that one I feel good about. And something else I feel good about?"

"What?"

"The rest of the night. Starting right now." He pulled her into his arms and onto his hard chest so abruptly she squeaked in surprise before he tunneled his fingers into her hair and kissed her breathless.

CHAPTER TEN

"YOU KNOW, MAYBE I'm feeling a little weak after all," Daniel said as he moved his hot mouth across her cheek and down her throat.

What did he mean by that? She lifted her head to look at his eyes through the darkness. Was he not feeling well? Or was he having second thoughts about kissing and touching her? Because the gleam in his eye looked like he was feeling absolutely fine. Very, very fine.

"What's wrong?"

"Feeling weak from kissing you. From tasting that beautiful mouth of yours." One hand reached to cup her neck, bringing her mouth hard against his, stealing her words and her breath. Never would she have dreamed that the tough, hard-eyed surgeon barking orders in the OR could be such an incredible kisser. Her head felt light, her body hot as she leaned into him, giving and taking.

When his mouth left hers again, she felt bereft. Until she felt his hands at the top of the zipper at the back of her dress.

"I don't think I've mentioned how beautiful you look in a dress. I nearly ran off the road driving here, looking at your bare legs and soft skin."

"And I don't think I've mentioned how handsome you look in a button-down shirt and dress pants that fit your rear really, really well," she breathed. "Much better than loose scrubs. Though I admit you do for scrubs what not many other men can do."

A short laugh left his lips, and she barely noticed that they were moving now, as he rolled them off the bed to stand up. Her legs felt a little wobbly and she was thankful he kept his arms around her.

"Thing is, as much as I enjoy seeing you in that dress, I want to see you out of it even more."

It seemed she'd barely blinked before she felt a cool rush of air against her back, his talented surgeon's fingers having unzipped her dress in a flash. It had been so long since she'd made love with a man, and always felt conscious of the extra few pounds she felt she should lose, but somehow, at that moment, nothing bothered her. All she wanted was to feel his skin beneath her hands, feel his body against hers, feel everything there was to feel with the unexpected flash fire exploding between the two of them. That fire that had smoldered for days, and now made her feel like she was burning up with wanting him.

With her heart pounding hard in her ears, she reached for the buttons of his shirt, fumbling to undo them. Daniel grasped the fabric of her dress and pulled it off and down, his mouth dropping to her breasts and licking them through the thin lace of her bra. His fingers shoved down her panties and she kicked them off, loving the low groan that came from his throat and vibrated against her nipple.

"I've wanted to touch these, feel these, since the very first day I met you." His lips teased across her breast, back and forth, until she was trembling with the goodness of it. "You have an incredible body, Annabelle."

Her hands clutched the back of his head, holding him to her. "You looked at my breasts while planning to get me fired?"

"Yes. What can I say? You're sexy as hell."

"I guess I should be glad you didn't come on to me before everything happened. That would have made me even more mad."

His teeth lightly bit her nipple and she gasped before those clever fingers undid her bra and slipped it down her arms. "I may be an ass sometimes, but I'm never unethical, even when I want to be."

His mouth moved back to hers in a deep kiss, claiming and coaxing, making her quiver and burn and fall further under his spell. She felt dizzy with it, barely aware of him leaning over to flick the plump coverlet back. She didn't know when he'd managed to shuck his shirt, pants and shoes, until she saw him standing there gloriously naked, his wide, muscular chest covered with soft black hair, his erection proving he was every bit as aroused and excited as she was.

"I want you, Annabelle. I've always wanted you, from the first second I saw you."

The glittering heat in his eyes made her quiver. "I want you, too."

He took that as the permission he was looking for and he picked her up and deposited her in the center of the bed, following her there to cover her with his hard body. He dropped his mouth to hers again, ending all conversation and thought. There was only feeling now—the sensation of his mouth moving across her skin, the feel of his hand on her breast and between her thighs. He seemed to be touching her and kissing her everywhere at the same time, and she felt mindless, like her body wasn't her own, like she was flying high in an erotic dream so intense she could hardly bear it.

Sensation overwhelmed her, and it was only when she felt his hard erection against her leg as he kissed her and touched her and made her writhe in pleasure that she realized she was doing all the taking and none of the giving.

She reached for him, arched into him, and he moaned, kissing her deeply for long minutes until he abruptly moved to grope in his bag, and as she was reaching for him again he began kissing her with a hunger she shared. Then he was grasping her hips, speaking beautiful Spanish words she didn't understand, and yet the meaning quickly became clear. Tender words, loving words. Her heart shook then melted at the beauty of the sound and the sensations. Until, with a single motion, he moved inside her, making her cry out with the intense pleasure of it. Sharing the perfect rhythm, her legs wrapped around him as the pace intensified and it was exactly what she needed, what she craved. And when they both shattered, the deep connection shook her body, her heart and her soul.

"So that's the whole concept," Annabelle said to finish her presentation to the hospital board, the mayor and a few representatives from Lima's education department. "Any questions?"

A few hands went up, and even as she answered, an odd, amazing calm filled her heart, despite the high stakes here. Of course she still wanted, so much, to gain approval for the project. But seeing Daniel sitting at the back of the room, smiling encouragingly, somehow brought it into perspective.

With any luck on her side, the various parties would commit their time, money and resources to make it happen. Looking into Daniel's eyes as he gave her a wink, she felt like she had a whole lot of luck going on.

But if somehow it fell through, there was always next year. A different school building or a different kind of building altogether. Maybe even a variation on the plan, an improved version, that would make the various players finally agree to participate. Last night had shown her that anything was possible and if something was meant to be it would happen in its own time.

After another half-hour it seemed there were

no more questions. Now it was a waiting game. Administrators would talk, study the research, crunch numbers and get back to her within the month. Somehow she'd just have to find some patience. And maybe a certain sexy surgeon could help her with that.

Chatting with some of the people there and saying her goodbyes, she sensed Daniel behind her. Then knew it was him for sure when she felt his wide palm press against her back as he came to her side.

"Not to rush things, but it would be good if we could head back fairly soon," he said, leaning toward her ear. "Apparently some patients are already lined up in Huancayo, and I need to get Alan and Eduardo there as soon as possible. But obviously they're still doing surgery in Ayllu right now."

She looked into the eyes she'd sunk so deeply into all last night and smiled. "I'm ready. It's either going to happen or it isn't. At this point, it's out of my hands."

"A remarkably mature attitude. I thought you

were convinced the world would blow up if you didn't make this happen."

The curve of his lips sent her gaze there and made her think of all the kisses they'd shared. Memories of which, with the presentation over, were apparently front and center at the top of her brain.

"Are you saying I'm not normally mature? I'm trying to put things into perspective."

"Since when?" he said with a teasing grin.

She almost said, "Since I started to fall in love with you," but bit her lip to keep from blurting it out. Whatever this was they were sharing, it was so fresh and new and wonderful, and since she had no idea where it may or may not lead, she wasn't about to tell him how hard she was starting to fall for him.

"While you finish up here, I'm going to talk to Carlos Loyola and the mayor, hoping they'll share something with me that they haven't told you. Torturing myself on your behalf," he said, flicking his finger beneath her chin. "Meet you downstairs in maybe twenty minutes?"

"Sounds good."

She watched him stride across the room to talk to the men standing in a small circle, and her heart bumped against her ribs all over again. Even thinking about the way he made her feel caused her tummy to roll and her hands to sweat.

It was scary. She didn't like feeling vulnerable, and up until last night had kept herself mostly safe. Had refused to dream of having more in her life than her work and her projects.

But hadn't she dreamed endless dreams as a child? And hadn't some of them come true? Was it so wrong to dream, then, that maybe Daniel could come to care for her the way she cared for him?

She wasn't sure. But she'd decided that she'd scrabbled her whole life for what she wanted. Maybe it was time to take that same attitude to heart again, to see if maybe there was something there between them that could last more than a day or a week.

His beautiful shiny black hair and his broad back in a suit jacket instead of scrubs kept attracting her gaze. Was wanting Daniel foolish or daring?

Either way, she was about to find out.

"I'm interested in being a silent partner in this venture," Daniel told Carlos Loyola. "What are the chances that the hospital and city will decide to participate? It's a big project, I know."

"It is a big project, with lots of challenges, I admit. But several of us are really impressed at the detail Dr. Richards has provided. Giving us nearly a turnkey operation from the beginning will make it easier for us to convince the powers that be to give it a try."

"I haven't yet talked to my family about becoming sponsors, but there's a good chance they'd want to." He glanced back to see Annabelle was still talking with people, her silky hair shining from across the room. "Regardless, I'm in."

"Would you be able to mentor students here?"

"I've been thinking about that, and I'm not sure how that would work, since I'm only here once or twice a year."

"In Chicago then? Oh, wait, you live somewhere else in the States, don't you?"

"Yes, Philadelphia. Though it might be possible to do some kind of mentoring there."

In the middle of the night, holding Annabelle's soft body in his arms, part of him had toyed with the shocking and unsettling thought of getting work privileges in Chicago. To see if there was any way he and Annabelle could continue some kind of relationship. Then he'd reminded himself of what had happened at the restaurant just before their incredible lovemaking, which had shown again why those kinds of thoughts were out of the question.

"What do you think it will take to convince the city and the education department here?" he asked, hoping to learn something he could pass on to Annabelle that would help.

"I think meeting and talking with Dr. Richards today is going to bring new believers," Carlos said. "She's so impressive, with her difficult background and somehow becoming a doctor in spite of all that. A woman who truly understands the kids we're wanting to serve is the perfect person to lead a project like this."

"Her difficult background?"

"Don't you know?" Carlos looked surprised. "Apparently she grew up in various poor ghettos around Chicago. Her mother was an alcoholic drug addict, and I'm told she was homeless half the time. That she was able to escape all that through hard work and determination is incredibly impressive."

Stunned, he turned to slowly stare at Annabelle. At her warm smile and sharp intelligence.

She'd grown up in poverty? Had been homeless? And with a mother she obviously couldn't depend on? It was unfathomable.

"Yeah, that is impressive." His mind mostly on Annabelle, he managed to say his goodbyes. "I'll be back in a couple months to finalize my participation in the project if it goes through."

The drive back to Ayllu was filled with conversation about the presentation and conjecture about the odds of it really happening. The more they talked, the more he found what Carlos had said to be incredible. Possibly unbelievable.

Maybe he was wrong somehow. Maybe rumors had swirled around about someone else, and Carlos had gotten them confused with Annabelle. Or maybe she really was the amazing person she was, times ten, to have overcome all that.

In spite of their history, he'd been grudgingly impressed with her medical skills since the first days of this mission, and that admiration had only grown as they performed ever more difficult surgeries together. Her Med Mission Wishes project was such a great idea that she'd not only conceived but made happen. Her charter schools and exchange student project, and the incredible amount of work she'd put into the research and presentation, were extraordinary. And now learning this about her past.

Annabelle Richards was without a doubt the most special woman he'd ever met.

He needed to know for sure, if only to understand her better. Since she'd never talked about it, he had to assume she didn't want to. And because he understood not wanting to talk about difficult times in your life, Annabelle being the only woman he'd shared about his brother with, he wasn't going to ask.

But one person he knew who he could ask? Jennifer. She would know. Maybe he wouldn't have a chance to talk with her one on one right away. But before the mission finished at the end of the week he'd make it happen, one way or another.

CHAPTER ELEVEN

DANIEL WAS MORE than glad that Eduardo and Alan hadn't minded going to Huancayo to work together there, as he'd have forced the issue if he'd had to. Apparently both men had somehow gotten word that he and Annabelle were involved, or maybe they'd just seen the way he looked at her. The way they looked at each other, when they'd both catch each other's eye then just stare at one another with hungry looks. He knew it, could feel the desire for her heat his veins and make his mouth water, but there didn't seem to be anything he could do about it. And he wasn't sure he particularly cared to.

Before the two men had left, he'd had to put up with some good-natured ribbing about it. He'd also seen Jennifer and Karina sending them sidelong glances and smirks, but as long as everyone was doing their jobs, gossip didn't bother him.

He hadn't yet been able to get the truth about the only gossip he was interested in. They'd been full up with patients every day, and everyone dined together at night. When he did finally have time alone, Annabelle was who he wanted to spend it with. Not skulking around the hotel, knocking on Jennifer's door to ask her a nosy question.

But with only one more day left on the mission, time was running out. And once he confirmed it with Jennifer, he planned to tell Annabelle he knew. That he admired the hell out of her. That the more time he spent with her, the more he shared a bed with her, the more he'd fallen in love with her.

His heart gave a jolt as soon as the thought came into his brain. But it was the truth. He did love her. He just didn't know what to do about it.

But now wasn't the time to worry about all that. He had a date with a beautiful woman who said she'd be out of the shower in...he glanced at his watch…four minutes. And since he had no idea what was going to happen after this mission was over, he wanted his hands and mouth on every inch of Annabelle Richards for as long as they were here together.

He moved toward the stairs, hoping to not run into anyone on his way to her room, when Jennifer came around the corner from the reading nook.

"Hey, Daniel. What are you up to?"

The gleam in her eye and little smile on her lips told him she knew exactly what he was up to. Or about to be up to.

"Just about to plan the last day of surgery," he said, even though he'd actually already finished it. "Can't believe we're heading home tomorrow night."

"It's been a fast two weeks. With a lot going on."

Again, that little smirk. He decided that now was the perfect time to find out if what he'd been told about Annabelle was true, and he moved closer so he could speak quietly.

"I have a question for you. You know Annabelle pretty well, right?"

"I think so, yes."

"I heard a story, and I'm interested to know if it's true." All the smirking was gone, and since she suddenly looked very serious and wary, he wondered if Annabelle had sworn her to secrecy. Or maybe she had no idea what he wanted to ask and was just being polite.

"What story?"

"I heard that Annabelle grew up impoverished. Was homeless. That her mother wasn't much of a parent. That she somehow emerged from that life by working hard enough to become a doctor. Is that true?"

Her steady gaze stayed on him for a good thirty seconds before she finally answered. "I guess it's okay to tell you, though she doesn't like it blabbed around. Doesn't want to be judged, you know?"

"So it's true?"

"Very true." Jennifer nodded. "She's incredible, to have accomplished what she has. Her mother was…well, quite honestly she was a drug addict. Alcoholic. Not around half the time, and when she was, you can imagine what kind of parent she was. Annabelle was pretty much on her own. They lived in awful, dirty, rat-infested apartments when they weren't in homeless shelters. But Annabelle was determined to become a doctor. And she did."

"I almost can't believe it," he murmured, his chest squeezing in pain for the little girl she'd been. "Who would ever guess that about her?"

"Nobody. And not only is she amazing, she's one of the most giving and selfless people I know. She's truly special."

Truly special. If he hadn't already realized that, this story would have proved it.

"Thank you for telling me. I needed to know."

"Be good to her," Jennifer said, her voice a little fierce.

He wasn't sure what to say, so he didn't say anything. Be good to her? She deserved the best, and to be treated like a princess. Could he be that person, with his flaws? Physical and emotional?

He shook off the disturbing confusion threatening to ruin his last night here with Annabelle, and headed to her room. After just one gentle rap the door opened to a beautiful, smiling woman wrapped in that pink robe of hers that showed off her curves.

"Hello, Dr. Ferrera. Can I help you with something?"

All thoughts from the past five minutes disappeared as he looked into her enchanting eyes. Stepped in and closed the door behind him. "Yes, you can." He reached for the tie on her robe and gave it a tug. Her lush breasts and soft, rosy skin still slightly damp from her shower were on display in all their glory, and his breath caught in his lungs.

He'd planned to talk with her, tell her what he'd learned and how amazed he was and how special she was. But the vision in front of him had him saying something else entirely.

"You are so beautiful it blows me away." He drew her to him and kissed her, let his hands glide over her smooth skin and cup her breasts and slide down between her thighs to touch the heat there. The heat that always burned between them flamed high. The rush of desire scorching through his veins nearly flattened him.

She wrapped her arms around him and moaned into his mouth as the kiss got hotter and wilder. All he wanted was this. To kiss her forever. Hold and touch her forever. Be with her forever.

Feeling dizzy and light-headed, he started to move the two of them toward the bed. But his legs didn't feel like they were working quite right, and he broke the kiss because he felt like he needed some air. Sweat prickled his skin, and his chest suddenly felt like a rottweiler was sitting on it.

Oh, no. No.

He tried to focus on Annabelle, but her surprised blue eyes seemed to fade away into sparkles. He blinked hard and fell to his knees before he realized what was going to happen.

"Daniel!"

Her voice seemed to be coming from far away and he tried again to get air. "Meds. My meds."

Vaguely aware that she left his line of sight, he

toppled over onto his side and closed his eyes, willing himself to not completely faint.

God, this was terrible. Poor Annabelle. Running off to get his medicine for a second time in a matter of days.

Focus. He had to stay focused so he didn't scare her any more than he already had.

The door creaked on its hinges again. "Here. Let me get you some water."

Aware of her rushing to the bathroom, he just couldn't seem to move. Couldn't open his eyes. Then she was there again; he couldn't see her but felt her fingers beneath his chin, holding his head up. Poking pills into his mouth, followed by a dribble of water. He swallowed, wanting this to be over. Over for Annabelle. Over so she wouldn't be scared.

"I'm going to take your pulse. Hold on. You're going to be okay. You know I love you, right? I love you. So much."

Love. She loved him. Loved him like he loved her.

He could hear the fear in her voice. Didn't want

her to feel that way over him. Didn't want her to love him and have to be scared to love him.

"Tachycardia, like last time," she said, her voice a tense wobble. "Meds helped pretty fast then, didn't they?" He still couldn't see her but felt her lips on his forehead and eyelids, her hands stroking his cheeks, his hair. "Just hang in there. You're going to be okay. You hear me? You're going to be okay."

Maybe. Probably. Probably he'd be okay. But he never knew for sure. He just didn't know. This could be it. Or the next time.

He saw it then, for certain. He couldn't let Annabelle love him. Had to protect her from that kind of pain. Had to stop what had grown between them. Had to make her leave. No matter how much it hurt to let her go.

The last day of surgeries had been nothing like all the prior ones. Probably because the mood in the OR was tense. Grim, even.

Daniel knew it was all because of him. Everyone had freaked out over his episode last night.

Everyone was worried, thinking he shouldn't be working. He knew he was perfectly fine, but that was part of the problem, wasn't it? Once people saw what his arrhythmia events were like, they tended to walk on eggshells around him for a while. Sometimes even treated him like he had a handicap or something.

Which he supposed he did, in a way. The truth was he was prevented from living a completely normal life because he just never knew when something might happen or go wrong.

As far as he was concerned, he was glad his tricky heart had acted up again. The intensity of it had smacked him in the head and made him see, all over again, what he'd known but had wanted to forget after falling for Annabelle.

Thinking about it now, he couldn't believe he'd thought his attraction to her was all about lust, and nothing more.

She was so much more than her body and her smarts and her smile. So much more than a woman to have a short fling with. He wanted her in his life every day. Wanted to hold her and be with her and love her.

The thought of never seeing her again made him physically hurt. Telling her the truth of just how bad his condition could get and the very real possibility his life would be cut short was out of the question. A nurturing, caring woman like her would never accept his uncertain health as a reason to not be together. She'd want to be there for him. Insist on it.

But it wouldn't be fair to let her love him. He couldn't do that to her. She deserved so much more. He loved her too much to saddle her with a man who couldn't promise whether he'd live fifty years or fifty days.

She'd lived with uncertainty her whole life, not knowing from day to day what would be coming next. The last thing she needed was more of that.

The weight of all that felt unbearable as he snapped his suitcase closed, ready to head to his grandparents' house for a few days. Just before he turned to the open door of his hotel room, there was a soft knock.

"Anybody home?"

Her sweet voice and beautiful eyes made his throat close as he opened the door. "Not for long. You packed?"

"Yes." She closed the gap between them, reaching for him, and he let himself fold her close this one last time. "How are you feeling?"

"Fine, which is the answer I gave you last time you asked." But he wasn't fine. Not by a long shot.

Her arms tightened around him, and the feel of her warm body against his made him ache with love for her. Made it too easy to forget reality and fall into the dream.

A dream of being with her forever, however long that would be.

Unspoken words of love tasted bittersweet on his tongue. Words that rose in his throat, but he managed to stuff them down. He held her close for another long moment then somehow found the strength to let her go.

"I'm heading to my grandparents' place for a few days, so I won't be going to the airport with the rest of you."

"You're not? Why didn't you tell me this before?"

"Didn't think it was important, since the mission trip is over."

He saw the confusion in her eyes and steeled himself against it.

"I thought that…we'd see each other in the States." She gave him a lopsided smile. "There are plenty of direct flights from Chicago to Philadelphia. I might need to come for one of your amazing massages."

"I'm going to be really busy with work but, who knows, maybe we'll run into one another on a mission trip again. I'm glad we moved past our enemy status to a cordial relationship."

"Cordial relationship." The prior warmth in her eyes changed to a cool, stormy blue. "Is that a euphemism for sex?"

God, he loved her spunk. Was there another woman in the whole world like her? He stuck his hands deep into his pockets to keep from reaching for her again, his gut churning with having to hurt her like this.

"Another thing I like about you. Your sense of humor." He put on a frown. "Are you mad about our affair? I thought you knew that's all this would be, especially as we're so *different*. Sweet but short."

All color seemed to leech from her face as her lips trembled, and Daniel was torn between wanting to get out of there and get this suffering over with, and grabbing her and kissing her and telling her it was all a lie.

"Mad? What would make you think I'm mad? A fling is all I wanted, too." He watched her turn and walk proudly, slow and sure, out the door, and each step away from him stabbed another hole in his imperfect heart. She flung her last words over her shoulder. "Have a nice life, Dr. Ferrera."

Have a nice life.

Without her in it, there was no possibility of that.

* * *

Annabelle sat on the hard airport chair and dabbed at the tears that kept insisting on puddling up in her eyes, angrier at Daniel with every tissue she went through.

"I'm not crying," she sniffed to Jennifer. "I never cry. Crying is stupid and worthless, just like Daniel de la Piedra Ferrera la-de-da-de-da."

"I don't know what to say." Jennifer was the picture of remorse as she patted her shoulder and handed her more tissues, and Annabelle was glad she had at least one real friend in the world. "I never dreamed that learning about your background would make him change like that. What a two-faced jerk."

"That has to be it, though. I mean, what else could it be? One day he's kissing me and holding me and acting like all he wants is to be with me, then the second he learns about who I really am, he's mister distant, I'm outta here."

"Maybe it really is that he just has flings, and then they're done with. That's what he told you, right?"

"Yes. But it doesn't make sense. If that was it, I think he would have mentioned it a few days before the mission was over. Put me on warning. But instead it seemed like the more time we spent together, the more he'd wanted to continue what we had."

Or at least that's how she'd felt, and humiliation burned in her stomach to think she'd fallen for a man she'd thought was warm and wonderful but who had turned out to be a shallow snob.

"Bottom line is he's from privilege and wealth and likes to help others through mission work and caring for the needy in his home country, but heaven forbid he should be involved with one of them. You know? And I'm one of them."

"Not anymore," Jennifer said. "Maybe it was like your college boyfriend's family instead. If Daniel's grandparents would disapprove of someone from a place like the Lima shantytowns, maybe he decided he'd better break it off."

"I admit I don't really know his grandparents, but they seem like very warm and nice people." Then again, so had Daniel, once she'd gotten past the stern, unpleasant part of him that often appeared in the OR.

"Well, it's his loss. He can date women from wealthy families, and miss out on the best woman in the whole world."

Annabelle swallowed hard, trying to believe it. But the truth was, she'd known all along she wasn't good enough for Daniel. He'd weaseled his way into her heart and made her feel like he really cared for her, but it had all been a mirage. A dream not meant to come true, after all.

CHAPTER TWELVE

DANIEL'S GRANDPARENTS SEEMED pleased that he'd decided to stay an extra couple of weeks, but he couldn't help but feel like when he'd been in college and had gone to spend spring break with them. Being coddled and plied with food as though he were still a boy and not a man, though he had a feeling part of it might be because they knew he was nursing a smashed-up heart.

He hadn't actually talked with them about it, but somehow they'd seemed to guess he wasn't hanging around just because he didn't feel like going back to Philadelphia. Being geographically closer to Annabelle would test his willpower. Hadn't she pointed out there were easy, direct flights between Philly and Chicago? The temptation might prove awfully hard to fight until he'd given his heart a chance to heal at least a little.

He stared out the huge windows at the ocean waves, remembering how amazed Annabelle had been with the apartment and the views. Intimidated, too. And now he knew why. As though what she'd done with her life didn't make her head and shoulders above half the people in the world who lived in places like this. He couldn't imagine that she felt that way but, then again, he didn't have a clue what her childhood had really been like. Obviously, incredibly hard.

Walking away from such a special woman, hurting her the way he knew he had, had him feeling torn up, inside out and upside down. The only thing he could think of to make it up to her at least a little was to try to grease the wheels for the charter school exchange student project, which was another reason to stay in Lima and work here for a while.

It looked like he was making progress talking with all those in Peru who'd be involved with her project, and he hoped Annabelle would get some good news soon. She wouldn't know he'd helped make it happen, but that wasn't important. What was important was helping her accomplish this thing that mattered so much to her.

"Daniel, I've brought you some breakfast. I hope you're hungry."

He turned to look at his grandmother, carrying a tray with pancakes and fruit, and more coffee, which he could definitely use.

"Thanks, Abuela. Are you joining me?"

"Yes, and your *abuelo* is too. Here he comes now."

They sat in silence for a few minutes until his grandfather started talking politics and his grandmother shushed him.

"That subject is enough to give us all indigestion," she said. "Let's talk about something else. Daniel, tell us about your friend Annabelle. Are you still seeing her?"

He stopped chewing and stared at her in surprise. Swallowing, he took a swig of coffee to buy some time because, as much as he missed Annabelle, he didn't want to talk about it.

"I guess that's a no? Or is it a yes?" his grandfather said in a joking tone.

"No."

"Why not?"

He tried to choose his words carefully because he wasn't sure exactly how to answer. Then simply told the truth. "She deserves better than me."

Both his grandparents stared at him, looking shocked.

"Why would you say such a thing? Any woman would be lucky to have you."

"You're forgetting that I have a hole in my heart." A second one now, though it wasn't one that would show up on an echocardiogram. "I can't promise her I'll be here for a long time. She's risen above tough challenges to become the most special woman I know. And she deserves someone who will live a long and happy life with her."

"A cardiac surgeon is saying this? I never would have guessed you could be so ridiculous, Daniel," his grandfather said sternly. "We are all human, and there are no guarantees in this life. You know that."

"Yes, there are accidents and sudden illnesses,

I know all that. But my situation is different. I had the arrhythmia episode here, then again less than a week later. I saw how worried Annabelle was, and she's had enough worries in her life."

"So you are playing the martyr and sacrificing yourself for her."

"I'm not playing the martyr." He stood and walked to the window again. "I'm just looking out for her."

"Do you think she'd appreciate this special way you're looking out for her?" his grandmother asked.

"No. But it doesn't matter. I won't burden her. I won't be the person to break her heart if I die."

"Perhaps you've broken her heart already," Cynthia said softly. "Let me ask you this. What if Gabriel had decided to run away from home so as not to 'burden' us with his heart condition. Would you have appreciated that?"

"That's a silly argument. He was my brother. Family."

"Is it? Would you have preferred not knowing him at all? Not having the years you spent together as brothers and best friends to protect yourself from the pain of that loss?"

Her words had him standing stone still, feeling a little like he'd been kicked in the chest.

Would he have wanted that? Would he have given up the years he'd had with his brother to have no pain over his death? No pain, but no memories either?

No. No, he wouldn't.

His years with Gabriel were priceless to him. He wouldn't give up one day of their lives together, no matter how much it hurt to lose him. He wouldn't give up one hour of the time he'd spent with Annabelle to protect his heart from the pain he felt today. And he suddenly knew, with certainty, she felt exactly the same way.

Appalled at how blind he'd been, how self-centered while believing he was thinking only of her, he knew what he had to do to fix things. If she'd ever forgive him.

"Thank you, Abuela. Abuelo." He kissed both their cheeks. "I'm going to Chicago to find Annabelle. I'll let you know how it goes."

* * *

Knee-deep in the boxes of supplies and equipment that had arrived from several hospitals for the Med Mission Wishes, Annabelle decided it was time to hand more of organizing this inventory off to volunteers. Maybe high school kids would want community service hours, and might be interested in being in the hospital and learning about all this stuff and what it was used for.

Pleased with that light-bulb moment, she figured it would be perfect to have some of the kids in the exchange program do it. That she'd just gotten word hours earlier that it was going to become a reality seemed impossible, but she was more than glad it was actually coming together. She was also more than glad she'd be even busier than she had been before.

Keeping busy was the goal. Too busy to think about Daniel. The man didn't deserve for her to be thinking about him. Five years ago he'd gotten her fired, and two weeks ago he'd broken her heart.

The jerk.

"I have a delivery for the Med Mission Wishes," a deep voice said from behind her. "Is this where it goes?"

"Yes, just shove it over there to the right," Annabelle said with her head still buried in a box. "On top of those green crates would be good. Thanks."

"It's odd how often I come upon you with your beautiful rear end waving in the air. The vision makes it a little hard to breathe."

Annabelle stood up so abruptly she felt light-headed. She swung around and stared, her heart bumping wildly in her chest. Hardly believing that Daniel stood in front of her, holding a large cardboard box and looking at her like he wanted to grab her and pull her into his arms.

"What are you doing here?"

"Bringing you a donation." The slight smile on his lips disappeared and he looked deeply serious. "I wanted to see you. Wanted to tell you I'm sometimes a horse's ass, but not a martyr. Or at least I don't want to be one anymore."

She let herself drink in the sight of him, even

as she wanted to walk over and punch him in the gut. "What are you talking about?"

"I didn't tell you I loved you when I should have."

Her teeth clenched and her heart hurt. Was this when he confessed about leaving because she wasn't good enough for him?

"You don't even know what love is."

She knew. Too well. It meant sleepless nights and tears and heartache and feeling like your life would never be whole again. But eventually she'd get over it. And maybe his being here, saying awful things, would make it easier.

"Until I met you, I didn't. But now I do." He set the box on top of the green crate, then stepped around a few piles and tried to grasp her hands, but she yanked them away. "I love you, Annabelle. But I wasn't going to let myself be with you because I convinced myself it wasn't fair to you."

"What?"

"You deserve more than a man with a tricky heart. A man risky to love, because I might be here a long time or I might not. I wanted to protect you from me."

He hadn't walked away because of her past? Because she wasn't good enough? Her thudding heart sneaked up into her throat and her gaze clung to his as she wondered what was coming next, desperate to hear it. "And now?"

"Now I've realized that's wrong. I'm not a martyr. I can't deny myself the privilege of loving you. Of spending whatever time with you that we'd have. My grandparents pointed out to me that the future for every single person on this planet is uncertain. I want my future, however long it is, to be with you. And I'm hoping you feel the same way." He drew her into his arms, placed his fingers beneath her chin. "I love you, Annabelle. Do you still love me?"

"Yes," she whispered, barely able to speak. "I do love you. I loved you even when I wanted to pummel you. I… I thought you ran out of the hotel and never looked back because you'd heard about my past. Because you know that I'm not good enough for you."

"Not good enough?" He looked stunned, then the darkly intense look she always saw during surgery sharpened his features. "And here I was thinking I was the stupid one. You're the most amazing, incredible, special woman I've ever known. If one of us isn't good enough, it's definitely me. But here's a newsflash. You're stuck with me anyway."

"Did you just call me stupid?" she joked to cover the lump in her throat and the joyful tears that threatened.

"Yes." He pulled her hard against his chest. "Let's both get smarter. Starting right now."

And then he kissed her. Long and slow and so delicious she had to grab his shoulders to keep from melting to the floor. When he finally broke the kiss, he leaned his forehead against hers and grasped one hand to hold it against his chest.

"Will you marry me, Annabelle? For better or for worse, in sickness and in health, until death us do part?" He tapped her fist against his heart, and her throat closed at the emotion on his face. "Never really thought about how big and important those words are, and even though it could be sooner rather than later, I'm begging you to say yes."

"Yes." She opened her hand to press it to his firm chest, feeling his heart thumping hard against her palm. "Yes, I'll marry you and all your imperfections, and hope you can live with my imperfections. There's just one thing I have to ask."

"What's that?"

"Could that for better or for worse not include getting me fired again? Because that was really awful."

"That's one thing I can promise that won't happen." He laughed as he brought her mouth to his again. "For better, worse and working hand in hand for the rest of our lives."

* * * * *

LET'S TALK

Romance

For exclusive extracts, competitions and special offers, find us online:

f facebook.com/millsandboon

⊙ @millsandboonuk

🐦 @millsandboon

Or get in touch on 0844 844 1351*

For all the latest titles coming soon, visit millsandboon.co.uk/nextmonth